Are You Married to a Psychopath?

by Nadine Bismuth

translated by Donald Winkler

McArthur & Company
Toronto

First published in English in Canada in 2010 by
McArthur & Company
322 King Street West, Suite 402
Toronto, Ontario
M5V 1J2
www.mcarthur-co.com

Library and Archives Canada Cataloguing in Publication

Bismuth, Nadine, 1975-
Are you married to a psychopath? / Nadine
Bismuth ; translated by Donald Winkler.

Translation of: Êtes-vous marié à un psychopathe?
Short stories.
ISBN 978-1-55278-869-1

I. Winkler, Donald II. Title.

PS8553.I872E8313 2010   C843'.54   C2010-903948-3

The publisher would like to acknowledge the financial support
of the Government of Canada through the National Translation Program
for Book Publishing, for our translation activities, and Canada Book Fund
and the Canada Council for our publishing activities. The publisher
further wishes to acknowledge the financial support of the Ontario
Arts Council and the OMDC for our publishing program.

Text design and composition by Tania Craan
Cover illustration *Wing Walkers* by Stephen Ibbott
Printed in Canada by Webcom

10 9 8 7 6 5 4 3 2 1

... the conversation we're having now would be unthinkable for our parents. They never discussed things at night, but slept soundly. But our generation sleeps badly, we are restless and feel we can find the answers to everything, whether we're right or wrong.   Chekhov

contents

FED UP YET?

We are everywhere. At the office, in the grocery store, on the elevator, on bridges, in cars, at the museum, in the subway, on our balconies, on our bikes, at the bank, at the airport. Whether we're PhDs, autodidacts, brunettes, redheads, thin, fat, jewellers, bureaucrats, lawyers or radio hosts, it doesn't matter. We are single. Fed up yet? We've been fed up for aeons.

And yet: goddesses, we would drive the Olympian gods mad; sirens, we would make monarchs of the waves lose their bearings. But it's all gone wrong. We've become virgins, witches, nuns, courtesans, governesses, tuberculars, unwed mothers, and old maids with cats. These days we inspire soppy novels and some with a comic bent (ha ha), films with an urban setting, prime time television series, books on personal growth, blogs, names for martinis, but mostly we inspire pity: we're sweet and nice, by gosh often even pretty, we're funny and smart, so damn it what's the rub? Why are we alone? An unresolved conflict with our fathers? Some trauma in our mothers' wombs? If you find the answer hand it over, please. Our shrinks cost far too much.

Our fondest dream is to meet a man, and we're not shy about saying so. We boldly proclaim it to our brothers, sisters, colleagues, friends, neighbours, to our butcher and our aesthetician, and we certainly don't have to repeat it to our shrink, but we're so bereft of pride that we even confess it to our ex, careful to frame it in such a way that he won't get the idea we're thinking of him. More than ever, we're ready to welcome a man into our life. But since everyone seems to have other priorities, we often conclude that it's better to take the initiative ourselves. We register on Internet dating sites and draw up a profile sparkling with wit, declaring our desire to establish a serious relationship with a serious male. We're inundated with replies, the "You swallow, you?", the "Are you rich?", and the "Send me a picture of your tits," plus a wealth of spelling mistakes. You find that scary? We'll spare you the worst. That's why we often resort to a venerable strategy that in forty or fifty years has still not proved its worth, but you have to stay upbeat, after all: we go out to the bars. You don't find the best merchandise in these drunkards' dens, but at least we can inspect it *in visu*. Saturated in alcohol, we might even top off the evening with some stranger. You find that imprudent? You've been watching too many corny thrillers on TV. Mr. Anonymous rubs himself up against us, divests us furiously of our panties but not our dress, then discovers that beer doesn't just soften the brain. Besides, this scenario is of rare occurrence; usually we end the night over a poutine without even having to worry about gaining a gram, because who will be there the next morning to prevent us from fasting for three days or taking a radical grapefruit juice cure? Who? Our cat, maybe? You? Certainly not, and certainly not the man we're ready to usher into our lives and who's taking his time, his bloody time, and it's too bad because these are our very best years and we'd really like him to turn up before the law of gravity really kicks in.

But we won't get discouraged, because if it's happened to others, why not us? There are stories going the rounds: in a law office downtown there's a man whose fiancée is the screensaver on his computer; in a swank neighbourhood on the mountain there's a man who's asked his girlfriend to move in with him; not far from the North Pole there's a man who ordered Jamie Oliver's books on Amazon.com so he could cook delicious meals for his loved one. Yes, there is, always, somewhere, a man who-who-who, and although these tales are wonderfully motivating, it's hard not to view them as legends. It's a bit like the famous deodorant that's supposed to not stain our black dress with white rings; you hear about it, it apparently exists and really works, but you can't find it anywhere. You don't believe us? We swear.

Because the unthinkable, the undreamt of, the unexpected – God help us, the miracle! – sometimes comes to pass. We meet a man and we feel that our turn has come: he's the one. Yes. This time, that's it. Jorge (if you please: pronounce it *Hor-Hay*, and roll the *r* properly against your palate) is our sailboard instructor in Mexico. We spend most of a week with him drinking piña coladas on the beach and making love in his shack where there's no electricity but lots of scorpions from which he keeps us safe, and once back home we take out a long distance phone plan and talk to him every day. Jorge and us, it's really strong. Love at first sight. So much so that he wants to come live in Canada. Of course, we know it's a bit crazy – what would he live on here? But we call the embassy anyway to see what we'd have to do to get him a visa. You think we're naïve? Don't be mean. You don't know Jorge. He's not like the others, and we're really hurt when he stops calling for no reason after he's said he loved us. Somehow you're not surprised, thank you very much, and you tell us, really, can't you find a man in your own time zone?

Of course we can. Because we can also fall under the spell of André (please, don't roll the r!). André is an old college friend we run into in the street, or the waiter at the restaurant where we hang out. With André we spend the good part of a week, and there's never been anything like it. We call each other ten times a day, we send him dirty text messages during important meetings at work, we go to his place at one o'clock in the morning and we spend weekends co-cooning which are so hermetic that our parents send out missing persons' alerts. Yes, with André, we re-invent happiness, until suddenly the penny drops. Surprised? You shouldn't be. Why do you think André was on his own when we met him? Exactly.

He's phobic (where commitment is concerned), narcissistic, neurotic, alcoholic or melancholic, in short a pathological case requiring therapeutic care, so it's best to take a powder before getting too involved, no? Well, yes. Of course, André is not always as bad as all that. You don't necessarily have to cite a mental illness in order to validate a rupture. Sometimes, what rubs us the wrong way with André after a few weeks, what he doesn't understand, is that we don't like him to go into our fridge and eat all the olives while leaving the pits to dry out on the counter; we find it disgusting that he uses our bath towel to dry himself off when we've told him to take one out of the closet; and yes, it gets on our nerves when he claims that the Guérande *fleur de sel* in our pantry is just for snobs and that Sifto salt is just as good, because no, we're sorry, it's *not* the same thing, and if he weren't so insecure, if he were more mature, he'd see the error of his ways. You say it's not the end of the world. But there's more: the problem with André, and we couldn't see it at first because we were blinded by our pheromones, is that he has no get up and go. He has no *oomph*. You don't know what *oomph* is? It's hard to describe. It's a *je-ne-sais-quoi* that excites us, lights our fire, makes our day, and when someone has no *oomph*, it may seem cruel to toss this out just like that, but it's kind of like saying that he's dull. Okay, no one's perfect. We know that André's only human. But he could be a more stimulating human, more sparkling, no?

You think we're asking for the moon and making everything too complicated? Ah, of course, we see you coming: you think we should throw ourselves at the first passerby, like really desperate cases? You think that because we're alone we shouldn't be allowed to choose? Didn't your grandmother ever tell you that you had to kiss lots of frogs before finding your prince? You say: but that's just it, haven't you already gone through all the frogs on the Internet, in the bars, in Mexico and here in town, and isn't that your problem? You have a point. We reflect: it's true that he wasn't so bad, poor André. Were we too demanding? Too idealistic? Maybe there won't be any more like him. Panicked, we call him back, but it's too late. He's thrown in his lot with Amélie. We're cut off at the knees. But we gird up our loins, we take heart; Amélie too will get tired of André's lack of get up and go. But the next thing we hear is that he has a hundred photos on his cell phone of their latest New York spree, that they've bought a condo together, and that he's making her *fettucine alle vongole* on Saturday night: isn't that *oomph*? But you don't understand. It's because André was with us *before* that he's learned to cultivate his *oomph*. We broke him in, as it were, we gave him his education. And screw it: *fettucine alle vongole* with Sifto salt, it couldn't taste as good as all that.

You find us full of contradictions, and to tell the truth, so do we. You start to lose hope in us. You almost think we deserve to end up alone, that it's not for nothing that our life is such a mess. This has occurred to us as well. We introspect, we question our principles, we dissect our mistakes, we decide to come to terms with our solitude. We take pleasure in watering our herbs and the tomatoes on our balconies, we plaster our refrigerators with our nieces' watercolours, we freeze what's left of our boeuf bourgignon, we take perfumed baths, we do crossword puzzles, sudokus, we do jig-saw puzzles with two thousand pieces, we go to bed early, we don't even answer the calls from Jorge, who's popped up again God knows why, and it's then that it happens. Just as our old aunts predicted, who turned out to be a lot more clairvoyant than our grandmothers: "You'll find someone once you've stopped looking."

And so yes, this we proclaim: we found him a little

while ago, and this time he's the genuine article. He lives in town, he's not a pervert, nor a drunk, he's no kind of –ic other than maybe fantastic or terrific, he has lots of get up and go, and he exudes *oomph*. The connection is super strong. We've never experienced anything so intense. What's his name? You really want to know? Since you insist, let's call him Jean-Marc. Jean-Marc who? You are nosy, aren't you? It's a bit delicate, you understand, or do we have to draw you a picture? Is it because he's over ninety that we're holding back? No, he's barely into his forties. And no, it's not because he's disfigured, either: if you saw him (ah, if only you could!), he's the spitting image of Hugh Grant. Stop scratching your head, he's not our first cousin either, holy cow but you are slow sometimes. He's already with someone. Now, are you happy? Jean-Marc is not exactly free, that's right, now you have it. Of course it's not ideal, but have you seen where that got us, looking for the ideal? Shrivelling up in our bathtubs surrounded by green tea candles, and trying to convince ourselves that that was happiness? It was just not true! Happiness, now we know, is Jean-Marc. Besides, it was always him. Even before we met him, something told us that this great backlog of disappointments couldn't have been for nothing, that it would lead us inexorably towards something unique, something exceptional, towards him, this larger than life man. Jean-Marc comes to see us Sunday afternoons and a few nights a week and we have fun with him, we have so much fun! We love him – yes, for the first time in our life we are in love, and nothing can stop it. Of course it's agony, we'd like to see him more often, and we'd like him to answer his cell phone even when *she* is lurking in the neighbourhood. But don't worry, that won't last, he's going to leave her soon, he told us so. You're exasperated? I see. You found us naïve and fickle just a little while ago, we earned back your sympathy with our tomatoes and our sudokus, but now you think we're frankly idiotic? My God, you've never lived, that's your problem, you're totally blinkered! Yes, he's going to leave her. If he really loved her like he loves us, why would he be between our sheets as soon as mademoiselle is off to her tennis lessons or out with her girlfriends? The secret with Jean-Marc is not to rush him, to keep yourself carefree and diverting. She gives him enough trouble with her "Where were you?" and her "You forgot to pick up my clothes at the cleaners!" As if she couldn't do it herself! This woman has no idea what it's like to be alone. A real griper, a pain in the neck. But don't go thinking we're just letting things slide with Jean-Marc. Oh no. We have our limits and there's no way we're going to twiddle our thumbs forever. Because it's true that waiting around is becoming our specialty, especially Saturday night, next to the telephone, with a bowl of ice cream. And yes, we know that the seasons are passing, in fact seasons play a central role in the ultimatums we address to Jean-Marc, sometimes out loud, but most of the time in our heads. Either we scream, "If you don't leave her by Christmas, it's over!" or "If you haven't left her by summer, you can forget I exist!" You think that even if our threats don't fall on deaf ears, the die is already cast, because Jean-Marc will for sure pull the same stunt all his life, and go cheat on us with someone else? You don't know what you're talking about, but if it makes you any happier, know that this possibility has already occurred to us, and it scares us to death. So maybe it's not such a bad thing to discover that the fulfilment of our dream is, it would appear, compromised. Last week, Jean-Marc told us *she* was pregnant – an accident, a horrible surprise, totally unexpected, it goes without question. But since there are no more tennis lessons for mademoiselle, or outings with her friends,

Jean-Marc's visits are increasingly thin on the ground, and his cell is less and less often turned on. We did, however, leave him a message the day before yesterday: "Yoo-hoo, stupid schmuck who couldn't care less where his genes end up, where are you?" We don't much think he'll call us back.

But what were we just saying? Oh yes. You see us everywhere: at the grocery store, on bridges, at the bank, at the museum. We are your sisters, your friends, your colleagues, your neighbours. Would you have a man to introduce us to? We are single. Once there were gods and heroes; we were goddesses and sirens. Then it all went wrong.

JET LAG

Jérôme arrived in a taxi on a grey April afternoon. My husband and I were at the living-room window. Our guest got his suitcase out of the trunk and Benoît rushed to the door to greet him.

"It's been a long time!"

"You haven't changed!"

I smoothed out the sheets on the sofa bed, I plucked a feather out of the pillowcase, and I went to join them in the hall.

Jérôme was a friend of my husband. He'd gone to live in France ten years earlier to work as a techie in the theatre. I'd never seen him except in photos. In person he seemed older. Benoît introduced us.

"Jérôme, Caroline."

We kissed on the cheeks and Benoît carried the suitcase into the living room. He hung Jérôme's leather jacket on a hook.

"Welcome to our home," I cooed, like a real hostess, while crushing the feather in the palm of my hand.

Jérôme said he was delighted we were putting him up, then he looked down at the ground and said we had wonderful floors. This trivial observation, dropped into the conversation just a few seconds after his arrival, convinced me that he would have preferred spending the week alone with Benoît. Man to man they could have eaten their fill, drunk beer, and treated women like enemies of the people. Because if Jérôme was spending ten days in Montreal, it was to get over his breakup with a girlfriend. In Paris, he couldn't get her out of his mind. He called her all the time. At night he crossed the city on his scooter to go ring her doorbell. Béatrice was the press agent for a popular singer. She'd driven Jérôme crazy to the point where he'd thought of killing himself and had to see a shrink. That's what he'd told Benoît in his e-mails last autumn, and that's what my husband, sparing me the sordid details, had repeated in giving me notice of Jérôme's visit three weeks earlier.

"They're pine," I said. "They crack at night. During the day too, but you don't notice it so much."

Benoît had turned on the coffee maker and he was washing the cups in the sink. I threw the pillow feather in the garbage, got some veggies out of the fridge, and went back into my office, a celery stalk in my hand. As I do translation for advertising, all sorts of urgent contracts pile up next to my computer. That day it was for a brochure being put out by a tire company that was introducing an anti-puncture product. Thanks to a new technology involving reinforced sides, this tire could keep on rolling for more than two hundred kilometres even when emptied of air. I didn't know quite why, but the principle seemed familiar.

Benoît had reserved a table at the corner restaurant, but when we heard Jérôme snoring where the living-room door was ajar, we decided not to wake him, and I made egg sandwiches.

"It's jet lag," said Benoît.

"Or emotion. Where's the mayonnaise?"

Benoît uncorked the bottle of Chilean table wine and poured us each a glass.

"It's true I've never seen him like that."

"He seems very uncomfortable with me."

"He doesn't even want to go to Saint Adèle to see his family. He told me he doesn't want to do anything, just walk in the city, go to movies, do mindless stuff."

I thought for a moment.

"Did you tell him?"

I rinsed the plates and without flinching Benoît poured some more wine.

"I know you told him."

"Of course I told him, he's my friend. What difference does it make?"

"The difference it makes is that he looks at me as though he's embarrassed."

"Jérôme has enough on his mind dealing with his own life. He's certainly not up to paying attention to other people's idiocies."

"Idiocies? You nearly went off with her. To her little unheated two and a half in Hochelaga-Maisonneuve. Your life would have been so romantic."

"And how is it with you, my life?"

Before going to bed I took a towel out of the wardrobe and left it on the kitchen table for Jérôme.

It only took me three tries to find the password for my husband's computer. My name and his didn't work, but that of his favourite writer flung wide the door to his personal correspondence. Her name was Katie. She made lots of spelling mistakes, and, to judge by her immoderate use of punctuation marks, she must have thought they'd been invented just to smile, grimace, and wink. I figured she must be a lot like those adolescent girls I sometimes see on the subway: plump, with low-hung jeans offering a glimpse of a polka dot thong, and a tight sweater running up just underneath her breasts to expose her pinkish navel. In the e-mails he sent to Jérôme my husband's disclosures were so puerile it was hard to believe they were those of a professor of literature. He spoke of Katie as a "delicious drug" and "a bird of paradise." Jérôme replied that in his opinion, passion was a mystery so opaque that it instilled in him murderous rages, especially when a certain Arnaud answered Béatrice's cell phone. A few days before Christmas, when the university administration fired my husband, he told me why, though sparing me certain details.

"You had an affair with a seventeen-year-old student!" I cried, shattering three glasses and two plates on the kitchen floor.

My husband went for the brush and dustpan, but the next day I found leftover shards even in the plant pots.

I pretended to sleep while Benoît was getting dressed in the bedroom, and I waited until there was no more noise in the apartment before getting up. The smell of coffee permeated the kitchen. Benoît had left me a note: they had gone walking in the centre of town and they would most likely be going to a film in the afternoon. They would call to keep me informed. On the counter there were two bottles of Bordeaux, and when I took the milk out of the fridge, I spotted the foie gras torchon. In the bathroom, Jérôme's toilet case was on the washing machine. I peeked into the living room. The sofa bed was impeccably made up, his towel was drying on the back of the chair, and a dog-eared paperback was sitting on his suitcase. I wondered whether Jérôme had left everything so neat because Benoît had told him I had at first opposed his visit, and he was trying to be as discreet as possible. It's not that I wanted at all costs to protect my intimacy with my husband. But that a couple adrift finds nothing better to do than to give sanctuary to someone who wants to salve his wounded heart, isn't that pushing hospitality a bit far? Besides, since Jérôme was aware of our situation, how could he hope to find comfort beneath our roof? The picture that came to my mind was that of a beggar looking for handouts in the poorest part of a big city. And in any case, did I seek refuge with other people when I learned my husband was cheating on me? I wasn't all that pleased to have a male version of myself camping in my living room. My husband insisted: "It will do us good to have some company." He tacked on something else about putting space between ourselves and our feelings, and then he ended by saying that in any case it was too late. Jérôme had bought his plane ticket.

Because anti-puncture tires were an invention that saved drivers from being stuck in the middle of the night trying to install a spare by the side of a dangerous road, the main advantage in putting them on one's car was security. The phone rang.

"Hello."

Silence.

"Hello?"

"Yes, hello," said a woman with a French accent. "Sorry to disturb you like this. I... I'm a friend of Jérôme. Is he there?"

"No. He's out with Benoît for the day."

"And you are?"

"Benoit's wife."

"Is there any way I can call Jérôme on your husband's cell?"

"He doesn't have one."

"Ah no?"

I sensed the growing irritation in her voice.

"It's Béatrice. Can you ask Jérôme to call me?"

"Béatrice?"

"Yes, he has to call me. Will that be possible? It doesn't matter about the time difference. Okay?"

I told Béatrice I would deliver the message, after which I could no longer bring myself to work. I took a shower and I went to do my errands. Outside the sun was shining and a few florists had put pots of tulips out on the sidewalk. I bought a lemonade at the little café and walked home chewing on the straw. Yes, I thought, me too, I should have left Benoît after everything that happened. Like Béatrice, who didn't want to have anything to do with Jérôme when he was in Paris, but was calling him now he was in Montreal, Benoît would have come after me for sure, wherever I went. He would have been anxious, worried, depressed. Sitting on the edge of the sofa bed, I watched the end of a documentary on global warming; we had to reduce our consumption of fossil fuels. Oh, why hadn't I left? To do it now would just be an impetuous gesture that fizzled. Absurd, because how can you be impetuous after the fact?

During the credits, my eyes came to rest on Jérôme's book. It was by a Japanese writer I'd never heard of. Absent-mindedly, my fingers pulled on the zipper of his suitcase. His pants, his sweaters, and his underpants were neatly folded. A bottle of antidepressants made a bulge in the inside pocket. I put everything back and smoked a cigarette.

"What do you mean, 'he met a girl'?"

Leaning against the kitchen sink, my husband was drinking a glass of water.

"I just told you. We spent the afternoon on the terrace of a bar on Saint Denis. The weather was great. Everyone was happy. Jérôme met a girl."

"A girl, just like that, and he left you there to go off with her? To her place? I thought you were going to a film."

"I don't know. I tried to stop him, but he wouldn't hear of it. He must have gone to the Holiday Inn. His plane ticket gave him two free nights there."

I imagined a room with a flowered bedspread, pastel walls, and double-glazed windows that street noise could barely penetrate.

"Anyway, Béatrice phoned."

"Yes. Seems they saw each other by accident last

week. When he told her he was coming to Montreal for ten days, she flipped."

My husband drank a second glass of water, then he came up to me to kiss me. He slid a hand under my blouse and caressed a breast. In the bedroom, the sun was setting behind the yellow curtains. We banged our thighs against the furniture and messily disrobed.

"You taste of beer," I said, but my husband replied that they'd drunk pitchers of sangria.

The rest all happened in silence. Then he went for one of the bottles of Bordeaux, the foie gras, and a package of rusks. He was climbing back into bed when the phone rang.

"It must be her," he said.

"Do we answer and tell her everything?"

My husband frowned.

"Let her get the voicemail."

"Is she insomniac? It's 2 a.m. in France."

" She's a neat kid. Very generous. When I went to see Jérôme in Paris two years ago, she invited us to Normandy, to her parents' home. I'm sure you'd get along with her."

"She was rude just now on the telephone. And if it was Jérôme?"

"He has his own keys. I told him to make himself at home."

The ringing stopped. My husband swirled the wine in his glass and sniffed it contentedly before taking a swallow.

"You know what, Caro? I was talking with Jérôme this afternoon and we came to the conclusion that it was a subconscious death wish on my part. I was deliberately committing the worst sin possible so that the university administration would have to throw me out. With all the time that teaching took up in my life, it would have taken me five years to finish my novel."

I turned the idea around in my head; I didn't like it. My husband's literary ambitions were to blame for this mess? I pulled the sheet up over my chest and the phone rang again in the apartment, shattering the silence.

"She's an obsessive, or what?"

"She must love him in her own way."

"You take her side because you're both the same. Except that you're a coward. You didn't leave me for catty Katie. She at least went off with her guy."

His knife thick with foie gras, my husband was slathering himself a rusk. In a nearby yard some neighbours were inaugurating their barbecue and

29

smoke from the grilled meat drifted into the bedroom on the breeze. When the telephone finally stopped ringing, I took a deep breath and swallowed a mouthful of wine.

"She's just nuts. And that's probably what he likes. You men always fall for the sickies."

"Will you stop? We were doing okay there for a while."

"Speak for yourself. And I'm sure Katie was neurotic too, already at seventeen. To have emptied a bottle of schnapps the night you couldn't go to see her because we had last-minute tickets for the theatre... Anyway, she's got a great career ahead of her as a pain in the butt."

Benoît put his knife down on the edge of his plate. He screwed up his eyes and tightened his jaw. I had a certain sense of satisfaction.

"How do you know about that?"

I bit into a rusk without taking my eyes off my husband and I took my time before swallowing.

"A-U-S-T-E-R. You should have found a more original password. Why didn't you just ask for a sabbatical? I knew about it two weeks before you got caught in the gymnasium. I read all your e-mails. I know that you even brought her here when I was at my sister's bedside after her hysterectomy. I wonder how you could have done that."

Benoît was pulling on his underpants.

"You invaded my privacy? You did that?"

"You couldn't take her to a hotel? You needed free time at the Holiday Inn, you too? Cheapskate!"

His office door slammed and I knew he'd gone to change the password on his computer. Outside there was also some slamming of doors, then the smell of grilled meat gradually dissipated. I woke up at ten o'clock. The phone was ringing again. I carried the plates and glasses into the kitchen, then I checked the voicemail; it was empty. In the living room, Benoît was perched on the edge of the sofa bed watching the news. A big American company had gone bankrupt.

"I'm sleeping here," he said.

Jérôme got back the next day at noon, which forced Benoît out of his office for the first time that morning. Our guest was in great shape, much improved. He'd stopped at the bakery to buy a baguette, some ham, and some chocolate éclairs. He left it all on the kitchen counter and went to change his clothes in the living room. I figured he'd taken a shower at the Holiday Inn.

"Did you make up his bed properly this morning?"

My husband shrugged his shoulders and I didn't say anything more. Anyway, I said to myself, what's the point of saving appearances? So what if the sheets on the sofa bed were messed up? I prepared some sandwiches and he made a salad. Jérôme came back into the kitchen dressed in black trousers and a grey sweater that showed off his pectorals.

"Béatrice phoned yesterday afternoon," my husband announced in the middle of the meal.

Jérôme sighed.

"I'll call her from a phone booth."

"Call her from here," said my husband. "It's only eight cents a minute."

Jérôme made a little pile on his plate with the cucumber slices.

"I left her your number just in case there was an emergency. Sorry."

"She must be afraid of losing you. She promised she'd try to make things better between you, no?"

"Promises, promises," I murmured while we were taking the éclairs out of their little box.

My husband glared at me.

After going through the film schedule in a cultural weekly, they went to see an American film that wasn't yet playing in Paris, and that was presumably rich in car chases and gunfire.

Once I was alone, I finished translating the brochure on tire manufacture, I took a bath, and pulled on a dress. I was watering the plants in the kitchen when the telephone rang.

"Hello."

"Jérôme please."

It was a girl.

"He's gone out."

"It's Camille. Can you tell him to call me? We saw each other yesterday; he has my number."

After hanging up I wondered if that's not what I should have done too: cheat on my husband to console myself, or to take revenge, or to forget. Whatever. I thought: but with whom? The fat tenant on the third floor? The waiter in the café who's young enough to be my son? With whom? I spilt a little water on the floor. There wasn't anybody.

That night at the restaurant my husband stroked my thigh under the table while Jérôme gave us a rundown of all the good things he'd learned from his psychotherapy. Attacking his roast beef, he affirmed that he could now distinguish the true from the false in his relationships with others, and draw a bead on his deepest desires.

"Are there desires that aren't deep?"

My husband told me not to ask silly questions. I shrugged my shoulders and told Jérôme that I'd already thought of going into therapy to treat my overall incapacity for happiness, but that I'd changed my mind.

"I would have felt like someone was poking around in my garbage."

"Anyway," said my husband, "there are lots of phonies in that business."

They argued over the bill, and Jérôme won. There was a full moon. We walked to a trendy tavern on Saint Lawrence Boulevard, where the floor was littered with peanut shells. Behind the billiard table there was a payphone with a red lightbulb over it, and Jérôme went to call Camille. Half an hour later, she walked in. She was a tall girl with brown hair who smoked non-stop without compromising in the least the lustre of her lipstick. They murmured sweet nothings into each other's ears and took a few turns on the dance floor along with some other couples. At a certain point Camille left, saying she had to work early the next morning. She was a designer for a fashion magazine. Jérôme went with her to the door, and I saw them kiss on the sidewalk.

"Béatrice is much prettier," my husband whispered, shaking his head.

"That's not always what counts," I replied.

He ordered three more beers.

Like a perfect tourist, Jérôme wandered around town all week, sometimes alone, sometimes with Benoît. One night when he'd been drinking, we took him to the casino. After an hour, as he'd lost four hundred dollars at blackjack, Benoît pulled him by the arm to get him out of his chair.

"Go fuck yourself!" Jérôme growled on the way home in the taxi. "I would have won it all back."

Béatrice finally called back on Sunday night. Comfortably installed in the sofa bed, Jérôme was reading his Japanese author. I wondered whether he was looking for some inner balance, as in Zen or something like that.

"It's for you."

He took the cordless and shut the door. I knocked three times on the door of my husband's office. He was sitting in front of his computer, where there was a yellow and black chessboard on the screen.

"My opponent is a ball-breaking Croatian."

Electronic noises spat from the speakers. I sat down on the old loveseat and told Benoît that Jérôme was talking to Béatrice on the telephone.

"So? She's not a monster."

"It's still because of her that he tried to cut his wrists."

"Jérôme told you that?"

"It was in his e-mails."

My husband frowned.

"You read his too?"

"Considering where I was at..."

I leafed through an old literary review that was lying nearby.

Ten minutes later the Croatian had won and Benoît swore while putting his computer to sleep. I stared at the metallic lightning bolts animating the black screen.

"If it were my name you'd used as a password, I could at least have thought it was a sign of love."

My husband sank onto the loveseat and pulled me towards him so I could sit on his lap. While he was inside me the floor creaked in the hall behind the door and we stopped moving, but when the steps moved on towards the kitchen, we started up again. Buttoning up his pants, my husband asked me if I really meant what I said the other night in the restaurant, regarding my overall incapacity for happiness.

"Eh, my love? Eh?"

I pointed out to him that it was time he bought some new pants, because those he was wearing were all worn. When we came out of the office, Jérôme was smoking a cigarette in the kitchen.

"She swore it would be all over if I didn't grab the first plane to Paris tonight."

He shook with nervous laughter while rubbing his neck. I put the water on to boil and I warmed up the tomato sauce.

"She's bored," said my husband. "You told her your return flight is the day after tomorrow?"

"She wants me to move in with her."

My husband opened the second bottle of Bordeaux and Jérôme helped me drain the pasta.

"You can stay here as long as you want," I whispered in his ear.

In the middle of the meal, as no one was talking, I asked them if they knew that there were now anti-puncture tires on the market.

"Do they make them for scooters?" Jérôme wanted to know.

"I'd be surprised."

My husband, who'd had to sell his Jetta at the end of January because he needed money, said we should beware of gadgets that go against the laws of physics. According to him, a tire ought to go flat at least once in its lifetime, or even better, blow out completely, because that's what confirms it in its identity. All its beauty is there, in the risk of being punctured, otherwise a tire is no longer a tire. I sprinkled a few crumbs of bread over my plate.

"Does that theory also apply to men?"

Jérôme cleared the table and allowed that it was complicated for everybody.

The next day my husband said he needed a cartridge for his printer, and Jérôme went with him downtown. It was dark in the apartment when I emerged from my office. The kitchen was silent with a late afternoon silence that made the very idea of progress seem ridiculous, even if the plants on the windowsills were green and glowing. I was in the bathtub when I heard steps in the apartment. I put on my robe. My husband was installing his new cartridge.

"You're going to print some chapters?"

"The first draft, maybe."

There was a Benetton bag on the loveseat.

"You bought yourself some pants?"

"No. Jérôme found a sweater for Béatrice."

I peeked into the bag and shifted the tissue paper. It was a turquoise sweater made of rayon. There were white beads on the V neck and the cuffs. The printer began to vibrate on its support and spit out sheets of paper covered with black and coloured stripes.

"Jérôme has gone to meet Camille," Benoît went on, happy to have installed his cartridge successfully. "He wanted to take advantage of his second night at the hotel."

I replaced the tissue paper and we ate a mushroom pizza in front of the TV. Then my husband went back into his office with a can of beer. I washed the plates and smoked some cigarettes. While making smoke rings, I wondered for how long I'd still be living with Benoît. In a year, would I be sitting at this kitchen table? At ten o'clock I went to knock on his office door. There were now some sheets of paper black with text on the printer tray, but he was playing chess.

"Are you coming to bed?"

"In a minute. I'm getting my revenge on the Croatian."

I saw the Benetton bag on the loveseat and I told my husband it would have been nice for him to have bought me a present, like Jérôme did for Bèatrice. I told him he was nothing but an egotist who cheated on his wife by sleeping with his students and would rather get beaten at chess than write the lousy novel for which he had supposedly sacrificed his career.

"Lousy novel?"

I unbuttoned my blouse and pulled on Bèatrice's sweater.

"What are you doing? Take that off, it's not yours."

"I want to try it. Maybe I'll buy one. Maybe I'll turn into a Bèatrice who'll leave you for an Arnaud. What would you say to that?"

I swivelled left, then right. The material was cool and comfortable.

"Frankly, turquoise doesn't suit you," my husband murmured.

I slammed the door.

When the telephone rang a few minutes later, my heart was still beating fast. My hand was trembling when I picked up the receiver.

"Jérôme's not here," I announced to Bèatrice.

"Can you tell him to call me when he comes in? I want to talk to him."

"Okay, but I don't know when. Do you ever sleep at night?"

"He went to see his parents in the Laurentinians?" I burst out laughing.

"We say Laurentians."

"Is that where he is? Where is he? It's after ten o'-clock over there. He must have told you our story. I screwed up, it happens to everyone. But he means a lot to me."

I wondered if I had anything to gain by telling Béatrice the truth. Did my suffering demand a victim? When was all this going to end? I gasped for breath and felt beads of sweat forming in my armpits and dampening Béatrice's sweater.

Around eleven o'clock the next morning, Jérôme came for his things. Camille had offered to take him to the airport. Through the living room window, I saw her waiting in her little rusted Honda. She was smoking a cigarette while blowing the smoke outside and tapping on the steering wheel. We helped Jérôme put his big suitcase into the trunk and told him he'd be welcome anytime.

"It would be great," said my husband, "a four-handed vacation, with Béatrice."

"By the way," I interjected, "she thinks you slept at your parents' last night."

Benoît looked at me wide-eyed; he seemed surprised.

"Thanks," Jérôme said with a smile. "But I would
have managed."

"That's what you think."

Beep! Beep! went Camille on the horn. Jérôme
climbed in and the car drove off. My husband and I
were left on the sidewalk. He put his arm around my
waist as the car disappeared at the end of the street. I
was at peace.

COME BACK, JULIEN!

Monday, 6:40 p.m.

This morning I went with Julien to the airport. He wanted me to keep his car this week so I could drive it to the garage and get the winter tires taken off. He kissed me on the mouth and promised he'd call me once he got to London. And if he were killed in a terrorist attack? He melted into the crowd and suddenly it was as clear as Baccarat crystal that you don't put in the dishwasher: without him my life would be a black hole. I felt like crying, "Come back, Juju! Don't leave me! I'll never get through the week alone!" I had a big lump in my stomach. Maybe I'm affection-dependent.

Or is it anxiety? Or yesterday's foie gras? It was a really big lump.

I was thinking about that when something very disagreeable happened: I couldn't start Juju's Lexus. All the drivers waiting at the departure gate started blaring their horns like animals while I kept turning the key in the ignition to no effect; the motor was totally silent. A taxi driver had to come and shout his head off at me that the engine was going but that it made no noise because it was a hybrid. Relax, my friend, how was I supposed to know? I usually drive a Mini Cooper. I arrived stressed out at my yoga class, my bamboo fibre top dripping already, and I parked the car in a delivery zone so as not to be late. Janet said, "Honey, are you okay?" She's really nice. We worked on my greeting to the sun and she told me I'd made a lot of progress in three months. So much the better, because even if I don't get the connection between inner harmony and standing on one leg with both arms in the air while staring at an invisible point out there in front of me, I'd be very happy if it made my buttocks as firm and rounded as hers.

In a sushi bar near Saint Lawrence Boulevard I ate a miso soup and phoned Véro to invite her to supper. "What would you say to a cheese soufflé with a little green salad?" She couldn't talk, she was in a meeting. Véro spends her life in meetings! For the last three months she's been "project coordinator" for a film festival. And she was supposed to call me back but she hasn't and it's almost seven o'clock and I'm a bit mad at her. I took the trouble to tell her that Juju had gone and she knows I hate being alone here. The house is too big for two, there are cracking noises everywhere, and I'm always afraid a killer will come in through the basement, the garage, the terrace, or (why not?) one of the skylights. If only Juju weren't asthmatic, I could have a cat or a dog to protect me. To distract myself, I had to go through my cookbooks looking for a menu for Saturday night. I couldn't decide between *carré d'agneau* and lobster. I didn't want to get caught at the last minute. I want everything to be perfect for the evening and... oh, it's ringing!

7:20 p.m.
Julien got to London in one piece. He didn't call me earlier because he went to supper with some clients. It's raining there. "And you?" he asked. "Me, what?" (I'm bored, that should be obvious.) Still, I confessed that I'd decided to try a new hairdo this week, to take a chance on bangs – like the saleslady I just saw at

m0851. "You'd be cute like that," he remarked, in a way that had me asking: "You mean you find me ugly now?" Of course, he said I shouldn't be so insecure. I suggested we do some telephone sex, but he was too tired because of the jet lag. I didn't insist. But I did want him to tell me how to turn on the TV. On the pretext that he'd already showed me thirty times but that I never remember, he made me take a piece of paper and a pencil, and I drummed into him again that I didn't like the new system. It's true. Since we got high definition, I can only see the actresses' moustaches and the hosts' acne scars. It kills the illusion. Juju sighed like someone on death row when I asked him again: is it the red button on the grey zapper or the blue button on the black zapper that I press first? We argued. That's depressing. I'll stop here. I'm going to make some muffins.

Tuesday, 8:30 p.m.

The problem with Véro is that she's unhappy at work, so I'm sure she's using me as a safety valve. She called me back this morning to invite me to have lunch with her, and that worked out fine because I had an errand downtown: I have to get hold of some Baccarat crystal goblets by Saturday night, otherwise Mme. Tardif might ask what happened to the ones she gave us at Christmas. In any case, I don't know what put Véro in such a state – ah yes, I know. It's when I called Fatima after ordering my cappuccino. I had to tell her to come a half-hour later than planned so she wouldn't have to hang around outside the door. "Who are you calling?" Véro asked. "My cleaning woman." That's when she made a face over her cherry-stem tea (she's trying to lose weight), nothing unusual about that, Véro's often in a bad mood without your knowing quite why. And because the only remedy to the situation is to behave as though nothing happened, that's what I did. I told her that Julien and I had rented a villa in Argentina for three weeks in July. Did she know that Buenos Aires was the Paris of South America? Would she like to take care of our house while we were away? She could use the swimming pool, the garden, the sauna, the cars, the gym, and the high definition entertainment centre. And so on, and blahblahblah. I really gave it my best, but after five minutes, as the expression on her face hadn't changed, I asked her if everything was all right, and she clenched her jaw and said: "I should really be asking you that question." She said I was living on another planet since I met Juju. She said I'd become a girl who spends all her time wandering around the Rockland Shopping Centre, doing yoga, and planning the arrival of her cleaning lady, and nothing constructive would come out of that. "You're living off a guy. What are you going to do if he leaves you tomorrow morning? Make a cheese soufflé?" I did my best to breathe from the gut like Janet was trying to teach me, to image the flop flop of the ocean waves so I would relax. But it didn't work and I got mad and asked Véro if she was calling me a high-class hooker. Véro answered that she'd never said that, but on second thought maybe that's what I was, because even if I wasn't mincing around in a fur coat and six-inch stilettos, everyone knows that to have time on your hands these days is a luxury, and where time was concerned, I had it to burn. What's more, it seems that I can enjoy whatever I like, but in the end, none of it belongs to me. My relationship with Julien is just a way for me not to face up to real life, not to take responsibility for anything, and what else? I forget because I blew up right in the middle of Java U. Do I have to feel guilty because I fell in love with the son of the president of the biggest aerospace multinational in the country, while she, all she's been able to come up with is an assistant manager at Pizzédelic (and even there, last I heard, he's still not ready to commit to her!)? Véro said that Julien's father's company was in *aeronautics*, not *aerospace*. "It's the same thing!" I cried. She threw fifteen dollars on the table and left, calling me a poor man's clone of Carla Bruni.

The bitch. I'm going to go bake a banana cake. Yesterday I burned the muffins.

Wednesday, 11:15 a.m.

I slept so badly last night that I called Mme. Lyne Gounod, head of Human Resources at the Fine Arts Museum. "Who? Myriam Boisjoli?" Just my luck: an Alzheimer's. "You remember, I gave you my recipe for apple crisp during the gala for the General Hospital Foundation." (It was in autumn.) Radio silence. "You were wearing the same Miss Sixty dress as me," I added. Maybe I should have said that I was wearing the same dress as HER, but on the spot it never crossed my mind. But finally, that's what got her out of her stupor. "Ah yes, Myriam! You're Monsieur Louis Tardif's companion, no?" I went right to the point: I'm looking for a job. She wanted to know what was my professional background, and I said a BA in Art History and two years as assistant at the Galerie Noir on Saint Paul Street (in fact it was only eight months, but if she'd seen the idiot owner, she'd know it should count for double). In any case, she said that unfortunately there was no opening at the museum for the moment, but if I were willing to take a test on general culture, my name could go onto the waiting list for the team of volunteers. I told her I'd think it over.

Okay, I can write it here – if I got upset yesterday afternoon with Véro, it's because I've turned the question around a thousand times in my head: what will I do if Juju leaves me? I mean, what am I, if not a woman at home with no children, and so not really legitimate? Juju, Juju... I just tried calling you at your hotel, but you were out.

Shit! I'm late for the tires at Lexus.

7:30 p.m.

I had lunch at Leméac. After two hours hanging around a smelly garage leafing through a paleolithic *People* (Jennifer and Brad on vacation!), I needed a break. And I thought I was cured! But everything started well. I was seated near the window, basking in the sun. Around me there was the usual chatter of businessmen and Botoxed ladies in retirement. But two tables away, there was a girl barely younger than I was. She was with her guy, not very well dressed, but rich for sure, because at a certain point he left the restaurant to get his phone out of his car parked in front on Laurier Street, and it was a Mercedes – the same model Juju was driving when we met. This girl reminded me of myself. I was certain that she didn't work either, otherwise what was she doing lapping up a crème brulée in a restaurant at two in the afternoon on a weekday? I said to myself, look at that, so I'm not an extraterrestrial! Other girls live like me, in a state of... what? Relative autonomy? Dependence on their boyfriend? So? It's not a crime. You're not taking anything away from anybody. What are we doing that's so bad, other than making other girls jealous, our best friends for starters. I think up to then everything was fine. But while the rich young slob was talking on his phone in the restaurant's lobby, the waiter placed the bill on the end of the table, and after eyeing the leather folder as though it were a dead bird that had fallen from the skies by happenstance, the girl drew it to her, rummaged in her brand new electric blue Rudsak, and pulled out a clutch of bills that she delicately deposited therein.

Perched over my duck leg confit – drier than usual, that was disappointing – even if I kept saying, "Well, to each her style of life," there was nothing to be done.

Suddenly I felt all alone in the world. My heart started to beat like crazy, sweat ran down between my breasts, my mouth was dry, and my ears buzzed. I had to get to the bathroom, but I was afraid of collapsing in a heap in front of everybody. I don't know how I made it to the cash and gave Juju's credit card to the waiter who was wearing Elton John glasses. Once outside I took the first taxi I saw, put down the window, and kept my eyes closed until we got to the Town of Mount Royal. Everything was spinning, spinning. I thought I was going to bring up. Or have a stroke. Or a heart attack. I thought it would be my poor Juju who would find my partly decomposed body on his return in two days and he would regret to the end of his life that he had left me all alone. I felt really dizzy, I didn't know what to do. Call Véro? Out of the question. My mother? She'd get too worried. 911? The neighbours might notice the ambulance, like that time Juju left for Geneva and I had to invent the story of a raging stomach flu when he got back, to cover myself. Because how not to fear the worst? A neighbour might run into Juju at the cornerstore one fine day and ask him, "I hope there was nothing serious wrong with Myriam the other morning? We saw her leave the house in an ambulance on a stretcher." Oh no! If he learned I'd stopped taking my meds, Juju would not be happy. So I called Fatima. I knew perfectly well that she was mad because I'd made her scour every cavity in my scorched muffin mould three times over yesterday afternoon – what can I say, I adore that mould, you can't find them anymore! But for sixty dollars, Fatima got over it and came by. I was hot, I was so hot that I was naked, flaked out on the feathered sofa in the living room when she arrived. I rolled myself up in the throw and she ran me a lukewarm bath. If my pill dispenser wasn't always lying around on the bathroom counter, Fatima would have thought I was pregnant. But that's not so. And why not? Because every time we talk about it, Juju says we're not ready. But when will we be? One of these days, even if I know it's maybe not the best strategy, I think I'll secretly stop taking my pills, just to show him he's wrong. At my request, once I was stretched out in the bath, Fatima agreed to stick around on the other side of the curtain to keep me company. Brilliant idea, oh what a brilliant idea! Fatima started to tell me that her sister, who still lives in Morocco, had developed breast cancer. I felt like crying, "My God, Fatima, don't tell me stories like that! Give me your couscous recipe, or something!" Couldn't she see that I was just coming out of a mega panic attack? Or was that her way of getting even for the muffin-mould episode? From behind the curtain I mumbled a few encouraging words, but I couldn't stop squeezing my breasts and finding lumps everywhere. After, it all got hazy. I wanted to sleep. I begged Fatima never to tell Juju what happened; if he asked why we'd given her sixty dollars extra, she should say it was because I'd asked her to deal with a big load of laundry. "You understand, Fatima? I have these little spells, sometimes. But I'm getting better." Fatima must find me strange, but what can I do? Anyway, she sees worse cases than mine, like Mme. Gray three houses down, for whom she also cleans, and who runs on Johnnie Walker. I signed her cheque and she left. What was it, five o'clock?

It's eight now. On the answering machine, a message from Daisy, my hairdresser: I'd missed my appointment. And me who wanted those bangs! I hope she has other openings this week. What else can I say about this awful day other than I'm again belching my duck confit? I'm going to fast tomorrow to have a flat belly when Juju gets back. I'm sure he wouldn't like it if I were fat. Meanwhile, there's still some banana cake in the kitchen, and as I put cream cheese icing on it, it's hard to resist. I licked the whole plate while writing these lines.

Thursday, 7:45 p.m.

Juju called this morning. Why didn't I just let it ring? I had to bore him stiff with all my problems. He doesn't want us to take tango lessons to get ready for Argentina; he finds it uncool. "But you can sign up on your own if you want," he suggested. "Let it go," I said. He's always just as rigid when we talk about children, and he wants to redecorate the house even less. "So what then?" I insisted. "We're going to carry on spending our evenings looking at actresses' moustaches on TV?" Talk about a shared interest. Juju said I was being a pain in the ass and that if he'd known he wouldn't have called. "Jeez, Mimi, I have four important meetings today and I just wanted to tell you I loved you!" That was all I needed, to feel guilty.

I'm overwrought. That's not good. I skipped my yoga class and went to pick up the Lexus on Laurier. There were three tickets on the windshield plus the one from Monday, that'll serve him right! Since I still had that lump in my stomach, without thinking, I dropped in at Véro's office. I needed her, but where was she? Of

course, in a meeting! I waited in an armchair in the reception area, it seemed like an eternity, I'd gone
through all the magazines on the table, and I'd imaged
more ocean waves flop-flopping than it would have
taken to sink the *Titanic*, when she finally appeared.
She greeted me less coldly than I expected, and it's just
as well because I burst into tears as soon as I was in her
office. I let it all out: that I don't know anymore if I love
Juju or if I'm staying with him because I wouldn't know
how to cope otherwise. That I miss the time when we
lived together in our four and a half in the Plateau
Mont-Royal. That everything's mixed up in my head
and in my heart. That I'd stopped taking my meds
without telling anyone because I'd hoped the yoga
would help me in a more natural way, but it's sure as
hell taking a long time! That I have no sense of accom-
plishment in my life. That God knows how I got there,
but I'm thirty-two years old and I don't even know how
to turn on the TV in my own living room. I would have
gone on for hours, it was so liberating, but Véro had
another meeting. She did, though, leave me an extra
key to her apartment, and said I could sleep at her
place if I wanted, from tonight, until I saw things more
clearly. I thought about it. It seems like a good decision.
I'm going to pack **my bags**.

9:00 p.m.

More lousy luck. Juju took off with the big Louis Vuitton.

Friday, 4:10 p.m.

I've just got out of the bathtub; Juju is still soaking. We had a great reunion. He's in a good mood because he signed an important contract in London. He didn't even squawk when he saw the four tickets on the kitchen counter. The jet lag has affected his memory though, because when I asked him what he wanted to eat tomorrow night, lamb or lobster, he didn't even remember that we'd invited his parents. And me who's run all over town looking for Baccarat goblets! "It wasn't necessary," Juju reassured me while I was soaping his back. "My mother couldn't have given you a hard time; she's already broken the crystal chandelier at the chalet!" I wondered: is that going to happen to me one of these days, too? You never know. Juju brought me a box of English tea. I prefer coffee, but I'll bring it out for visitors. Or I could offer it to Fatima, to console her for her sister's illness. Or to Véro, if there's one with cherry stems. I must call her anyway today to reassure her and tell her she should stop worrying about me. Actually, I'm doing very well. Things go all out of proportion when Juju's away, and that makes me question everything; it's only normal. But I hope she'll be in a meeting and I'll get her voicemail, because if she picks up I can guess what she'll say, something discouraging like "It's your life, Mimi."

Indeed.

Shit! I'm late for my hairdressing appointment again!

VISITING MADAME TROTTIER

It was Easter. Madame Trottier put a plate down in front of me: two thick slices of ham topped with cubes of pineapple with green beans swimming in a pool of melted butter. My gorge rose. As if that weren't enough, before going back into the kitchen, she said, "Eat it while it's hot, Karine."

I looked at Steve, he lowered his eyes. His sister Mélanie burst out laughing and the guy she'd brought with her asked what was going on.

"Karine is my brother's ex," she said. "She's super cool, but she went off to live with her father in the States. This is Julie and she doesn't eat meat."

She pointed her fork at me. "Pest," I thought. As Mélanie hadn't taken the trouble to introduce me, the guy stretched his arm across the table to shake my hand: "I'm Benjamin." "Nice to meet you," I replied, and it was true. He seemed pleasant, which is not always the case with the men my sister-in-law digs up. At Christmas her date bombarded us all night with hockey stories because he played in a college league. At one in the morning, with Madame Trottier asleep on the couch, he asked Mélanie, "Should we go into your mother's room?" Mélanie'd jumped up. We heard her shouting in the hall: "Gimme an S, gimme an E, gimme an X, what does that spell?" Mélanie's a cheerleader for her school's football team.

Steve grabbed my plate.

"I'll fix things," he assured me, before vanishing into the kitchen.

Mélanie put down her fork: "Gna, gna, gna, I'll fix things," she repeated. Benjamin smiled at me shyly, before asking Mélanie where the bathroom was. Once he was out of sight, Mélanie winked at me.

"That guy there is the fuck of the century."

"Neat," I said.

Steve's mother came back into the dining room with more plates.

"I'll warm you up some broccoli soup, Julie," she said, pronouncing my name's two syllables very distinctly.

Steve sat back down next to me and put a hand on my thigh.

As usual, I helped Steve clear the table. During supper his mother had drunk the two bottles of wine almost singlehandedly, and had gone back to calling me Karine. She said, "Are you sure you've had enough to eat, Karine?" or "Would you like me to open another can of soup, Karine?" Each time, Mélanie giggled and buried her face in Benjamin's neck.

In the kitchen, I rinsed the plates.

"She must miss her!" I remarked.

"She's been drinking," said Steve, while arranging the glasses on the top shelf of the dishwasher. "She doesn't do it on purpose, okay?"

I shrugged my shoulders.

Three days earlier, as I was studying for an exam with Steve, Karine had phoned. For Easter, she wanted him to have a dozen daffodils sent to the old age home where her grandmother was living. When Steve hung up, he told me about it nervously, without even looking me in the eye. I would have liked to know if Karine often called at nine o'clock at night to ask him for favours. But I just shrugged my shoulders; it's a habit I have when I'm out of sorts.

"My mother doesn't do it on purpose," Steve repeated.

I passed him the plates and said I was going to smoke a cigarette.

Given Madame Trottier's state, I could have smoked in the apartment without her knowing anything about it. Despite that, after having pulled my coat off the bed, I went, as usual, onto the balcony giving off her bedroom. It was drizzling, but the balcony overhead offered me protection. In front of me, attached to the metal bars, were two white plastic pots filled with earth covered in twigs from herbs yellowed by the winter. I admired the city, all its lights blinking. I wondered if Steve still loved Karine, and if so, whether it mattered. She was supposed to be staying in Chicago for three more years. I didn't even know where it was, Chicago: way in front of me over the city, towards the west, the east, or even far behind? They don't talk about Chicago in my nursing manuals. I wondered if I loved Steve. No one else but me could know.

"It's raining," observed Benjamin, opening the door behind me.

He scratched a match and took a first puff from his cigarette. He told me he was studying to become a chiropractor at the university in Trois-Rivières, and that he was finishing up a residency at a clinic in Montreal. I told him I had two years left to go before receiving my nursing degree.

"How old are you?" he asked.

"Twenty. You?"

"Twenty-five. But I would have thought you were seventeen, max."

"Yes, I have to show my card when I go to bars."

At which point Mélanie slid open the door leading to the balcony. After asking Benjamin for a light, she looked at me.

"Gimme a J! Gimme a U! Gimme an L! Gimme an I! Gimme an E! What does that spell?"

I butted out my cigarette in one of the spice pots and I left them alone.

Steve was rummaging in the kitchen cupboards.

"There's no coffee," he grumbled.

Madame Trottier was talking on the phone in the living room. I approached her and she raised her head, but she continued her conversation as though she hadn't seen me. Judging by her disjointed words, I understood that someone had been sprayed by a skunk while putting out the garbage.

"Tomato juice," repeated Madame Trottier.

"Excuse me," I interjected.

"Hey, girl," she said, squinching up her eyes, one hand on the receiver. "You want more vegetables?"

The coffee was in the freezer.

I went back to the kitchen.

"Talk about a place!" Steve grumbled.

While the coffee maker purred and the first drops were dribbling into the Pyrex pot, I asked Steve if we'd be going soon. He applied a kiss to my brow. "It won't be long." Mélanie and Benjamin joined us. Mélanie advanced on Steve and started to kiss him on the neck while tickling him and laughing like a kid. Benjamin kept his hands in his jeans pockets. He seemed embarrassed watching Mélanie, who wouldn't stop lavishing caresses on her big brother.

I was used to my sister-in-law's little games. I wondered what Benjamin was doing with such a girl, and I went back to smoke another cigarette.

But I had no desire for another cigarette. I stretched out on Madame Trottier's bed. It was a waterbed and it pitched and rolled. I wondered what Madame Trottier could possibly dream about at night when she was sleeping alone on this squishy mattress: her youth as a flight attendant or her former husband? Just over the bed there was a fan with four static blades. Outside, the sound of the rain grew louder. Somewhere in the apartment, I heard Madame Trottier moaning like a damaged violin. It's almost always like that when you visit Madame Trottier; either she's crying or she's sleeping. Rarely anything in between.

Benjamin came into the room. After having noted that the balcony was empty, he stood motionless in front of the sliding window. I coughed so he would see I was there, and he came towards the bed.

"Is it because they're going for brunch with their father tomorrow morning?" I asked.

"I don't really know."

As our coats were taking up most of the bed, Benjamin had to sit close to me and that made waves. He seemed surprised, then said that waterbeds were very bad for the vertebrae. But did Madame Trottier care about the health of her vertebrae? Her voice bellowed louder and louder through the half-open door, which was letting in a little light. Benjamin looked at his watch, then his feet.

"I've been going out with Steve for almost a year, and she still gets my name wrong," I sighed.

I turned on my side to look at Benjamin. He had strong shoulders and a muscular nape. I dug my fingers into the mattress. Doors slammed in the apartment and my stomach started to gurgle. I'd known what to call this embarrassing phenomenon for a while now: borborygmus. I put my hand on my stomach so it would quiet down.

"You must be hungry," remarked Benjamin. "With your little soup. Why don't you eat meat?"

"Because it disgusts me."

He stretched towards the pile of coats and looked for his own, which made the bed pitch even more. I let myself be rocked, and remembered what Mélanie said at Christmas when she came out of the room with her lunk: "Oof! Bouncy bouncy bouncy!" Benjamin rummaged in his pockets and pulled out an egg swathed in gold foil. He gave it to me and I unwrapped it.

"There was a big jar full of eggs like that at the clinic this week. I took a bunch."

"Thanks."

The shell was milk chocolate and inside there was a sugary yellow cream. I gulped it down in two bites. Then I made the wrapping into a ball and squeezed it in my hand.

"I think Steve still likes his old girlfriend."

Benjamin didn't say anything, so I went on.

"I'm a bit scared she'll be back for summer vacation. Is it far, Chicago?"

"I think it's just the other side of the Great Lakes."

That didn't mean much to me. I closed my eyes. The rain was lashing the windowpane. In the apartment, Mélanie was crying tearfully, Steve was telling her to calm down, Madame Trottier was wailing away. I opened my eyes and looked at the fan over my head.

"You want to kiss me, Benjamin? I kind of need it."

His breath stopped somewhere inside his rib cage. He turned and plunged his eyes into mine. I gently moved my pelvis and he watched me for a moment before turning again towards the ray of light coming through the half-opened door. He said I was special. I stopped writhing. After, we stayed like that on Madame Trottier's waterbed until we heard someone's footsteps coming down the hall.

THE WAITING LINE

That summer, word went around that all the couples were splitting up. From the alignment of the stars to the disappearance of traditional models, everyone had a theory that would account for the breakdown of the amorous unit. Dinners with friends ended later than usual, shoe stores were invaded by tired-eyed young women nattering into their cell phones, lines for bars reached into the streets, prompting petitions from the neighbourhood residents. On Laurier Street, a few metres from the entrance to B***, where there was a black doorman on duty with a helmet of dreads on his head, Bénédicte and Rosalie were waiting their turn.

"I ate too much," said the first. "I'm sure I've gained five pounds."

"You're imagining things," answered the other.

The two friends had lost contact since their vague Communications Studies at university, but they'd spent the last six Saturday nights together, because, as they were fond of repeating, "men are cretins." And yet, if they went out to B*** dressed in their fanciest finery, it was in hopes of meeting someone who would make them change their minds. The miracle was biding its time, however. Bénédicte had only managed to lure home a lawyer answering to the name Jean-Philippe, who made love to her while calling out to Valérie. "Valérie's your ex?" inquired Bénédicte the next morning. "She left you for someone else? You're sad? You want a coffee?" Jean-Philippe farted into the sheets, so he was able to dodge all these questions. "Oh, I'm so sorry, I..." He left without noting her telephone number. As for Rosalie, she had allowed a certain Normand, co-owner of a sports store (or was it a gym), to drive her home, but once at the wheel of his gleaming Volvo he got a call on his BlackBerry, and hanging up, asked Rosalie if she would very much mind going the rest of the way in a taxi. "There's a stand not far," he indicated, before stopping his car at the corner of Mount Royal and Saint Urbain. "Do you need cash?" Despite these uninspiring results, Rosalie and Bénédicte refused to be discouraged. "I'd prefer," opined Rosalie, "a guy who leaves me on a street corner to a guy who can't manage his intestines or remember my name in bed!" To which Bénédicte replied, "I'd prefer anything to being stuck home alone on Saturday night!" So although things weren't perfect, they could have been worse.

Bénédicte asked Rosalie for a light. She fired up a cigarette and breathed in the smoke with an air of exasperation. This look of impatience and superiority came over her face several times a day, and was characterized by a severe knitting of her brows. Bénédicte had taken to plucking her brows so fine of late that her forehead, when it contracted, seemed to swallow them up, turning the upper part of her face into a seamless mass of pink smooth flesh, with two little brown eyes poking through.

"How many times have we been here?" said Bénédicte. "He should recognize us."

Bénédicte took one step to the side, out of the line. She balanced herself on her thin legs, hoping to catch the doorman's attention. He did stare at her blankly for a few seconds before directing his attention elsewhere.

Rosalie returned her lighter to her purse, and took the opportunity to consult the luminous screen of her cell phone lying at its bottom; why the hell did it only give her the time instead of signalling a missed call or the arrival of a text message?

"He must be short-sighted," she allowed, shutting her purse.

It was a beautiful August night. A crescent moon lit up the sky and a warm, humid breeze was sweeping along some loose garbage from the sidewalk. Clients were coming out of B*** to take their cigarette breaks near a big clay flowerpot. The boys were dishevelled, the girls' cleavage was dangerously out of line, the conversations disjointed:

"Stéphane could kill you at tennis."

"Fuck you, he doesn't know how to drink!"

Bénédicte went back into line, shaking her leg where an ice-cream-sandwich wrapping had come to rest.

"Or maybe he's got amnesia," she sighed. "Do I have something stuck between my teeth?"

Bénédicte discreetly retracted her lips and displayed her bright white teeth. Rosalie took a look, said no, and asked for a puff of her cigarette. How much longer would they have to cool their heels on this bit of sidewalk? They should have known that the line to get into B*** would move at a snail's pace. They should have got away earlier from Geneviève's, her copy-editor colleague at the magazine. But how could they have? Geneviève took so long to recount each minute detail of her separation from Mathieu that they didn't dare interrupt her. There was Mathieu's ambivalent behaviour, Geneviève's disappointed hopes, the ups and downs of their relationship, Geneviève's constant need for reassurance, and finally, the nail in the coffin: Mathieu's ongoing reluctance to envisage their cohabitation. Only Bénédicte showed some signs of impatience: over the cherry pie that had succeeded the lamb fricassee, she cried, "If the poor little schmuck was suffocating so badly, you should have bought him a puffer! Now come out with us, it'll do you good!" But Geneviève claimed she'd drunk enough alcohol for one night, plus she had a rendezvous at noon the next day with a certain Hubert she'd met on the Internet. She even ran to get her laptop to show them his photo. "What do you think?" she asked. As though to justify her move, she added, "It seems you're supposed to get back on the horse right after you've fallen off." For a few seconds, Bénédicte and Rosalie tilted their heads to the left and then to the right in front of the computer screen so as to better take in the blondish kid with dark glasses perched on his nose, wearing a Bart Simpson T-shirt. "Looks like an overgrown adolescent," put in Bénédicte. "Don't bring him back to your place," offered Rosalie. But Geneviève was hardly listening, as she'd clicked on her e-mail icon to see if, by chance, Mathieu might not have sent her a heated message, asking forgiveness. There wasn't anything. Geneviève was disappointed – again. She accompanied her guests to the door, dragging her feet on the wooden floor in her little Mile End apartment smelling of tomato, thyme, oregano, and basil. "You sure you don't need help with the dishes?" Bénédicte asked, dutifully. "No," Geneviève sighed, her eyes moist. "Thanks for having come, it made me feel better."

Bénédicte crushed her cigarette under her sandal, from which protruded her scarlet toenails.

"By the time we get in, all the guys will be drunk or will have their eyes on some other girl. Or both."

Just then Rosalie, who was in the process of rubbing her new gloss stick over her lips, almost swallowed the tube: "Holy shit!" she yelped.

She swung around so her back would be to the street. She hid her face in the neck of Bénédicte, who raised her head and saw three boys getting out of a

Toyota Matrix. The tails of their short-sleeved shirts were wafting in the breeze, the rear pockets of their jeans were deformed by cell phones and cigarette packs; they crossed the street and advanced on the doorman of B*** who, in front of the half-blasé, half-offended crowd waiting in line, let them in.

"Is it Thierry?" asked Bénédicte, while trying to peel her hair off Rosalie's lip gloss. "Wow, that stuff smells good. Is that your ex? Is it him? Who is it? It's all right, he's inside. But what a drag, if you know him he could maybe have got us in."

The line moved a few centimetres and Rosalie took two steps, still cowering in the neck of Bénédicte, whose heady perfume was beginning to make her ill – a good reason for her to pull herself together. She shot a glance towards the Toyota Matrix which, contrary to what she thought she had seen, was not metallic blue, but white. She felt her muscles relax.

"I thought it was Zachary, Thierry's brother, But it's okay. It's not even his car."

"All right then," Bénédicte murmured. "Anyway, so what if you had seen him again?"

Rosalie made a face while picking up on the application of her lip gloss where she'd left off. How could Bénédicte ask such a question? Rosalie had told her the whole story, after all. Four months earlier, after Rosalie and Thierry (but mostly Thierry) had agreed that the day-to-day had had its way with their desire and had arrived at the shared conclusion (but much more Rosalie) that certain unorthodox practices were not up to reviving it, Thierry went to sleep at his brother Zachary's. "I need to reflect," he'd explained. "You won't hold it against me?" For five days Rosalie had resisted the urge to hold it against him, and even more (all her friends told her this was a real exploit) to call him. Wanting to reflect, Rosalie thought, wasn't that healthy for a couple that had been together for almost three years? Rosalie cleaned out all the closets and chests of drawers in their apartment, tucking lavender sachets into every corner, a herb well known for its soothing virtues. Still, she was becoming anxious. On the sixth day, at the end of her rope, she got Thierry's voicemail on his cell phone. The seventh day, because Thierry had not replied to her thirty-eight messages, Rosalie turned up at Zachary's apartment. He opened the door, two twenty-dollar bills in his hand. "Oh... Rosalie?" he blurted out, turning his head towards the living room where Thierry was ensconced on the couch. "I thought it was..." He was looking at her again. "Sorry. Our chicken." Pushing into the entranceway uninvited, Rosalie craned her neck. "Thierry? Come here!" Thierry was still dressed in his suit from work, his tie loose around his neck. Seeing her, he smiled thinly, then took a long slug from his beer. The TV was on; from where she stood Rosalie couldn't see the screen, but a breathless voice was talking about winning lines and checking. Zachary disappeared into the kitchen and Thierry came up the hallway. "Hey, hi," he said, depositing a limp kiss on her cheek. Hi, Rosalie repeated to herself, that's all he has to say? "How long are we going to go on like this?" she barked. "Are you coming home, or not?" Thierry averted his eyes. "I don't know," he stammered. "The game is starting. Can I call you tomorrow?" Rosalie's eyes met those of Zachary, who was coming out of the kitchen with two bottles of beer, his two bills now sticking out of the front pocket of his jeans. The television voice droned on: "*Number 17 is showing more maturity on the ice...* " Rosalie remained planted there, not knowing what to do. Even though almost a week had gone by since Thierry had left, she'd still not understood until now that it was all over between them. And so her "blockage" (Thierry's word) had done them in as a couple. But Rosalie was too shaken to accept this state of affairs. Besides, when she later described the scene to her friends, she couldn't find any better way to put it than that she was in a kind of "twilight zone." "Come home," she kept saying, her voice verging on hysteria. "Come home with me! Come home!" Thierry gathered Rosalie up in his arms. "Don't make things harder. I've got a lot of respect for you. But I have to listen to my own voice. We're just not right for each other on that level." Rosalie pushed Thierry away and tore down the front steps. Just as she was getting into her car, the chicken man emerged from his, a bright yellow sub-compact. "Excuse me," said Rosalie. "Yes?" said the deliveryman. He was about thirty years old with a hearty appearance, a healthy complexion, and an affable manner, but the particular situation in which she found herself blinded her to all of that. Without skipping a beat, she grabbed hold of the two cardboard boxes he was carrying; their colour matched his car, and they were tied together with string. She threw them to the ground and stomped on them, oblivious to the deliveryman's wail: "Holy Christ!" From the top of the steps, Thierry and Zachary observed the scene, stunned. "I just don't get it!" cried Rosalie, giving one more kick to a Styrofoam cup. "I don't, I don't, I don't!" "Christ Almighty," whined the deliveryman. Once in her car, Rosalie took a Kleenex out of her bag and sponged the dribbles of brown sauce from her high heels along with the residue of French fries, chicken skin, and coleslaw, before bursting into tears. Three days later, after she'd scoured them with a horsehair brush, sprayed them with silicone, and even sprinkled them with essence of lavender, her shoes still reeked of barbecued fowl, which gave her an excellent excuse to buy a new pair, prettier and more expensive, in Italian leather. Rosalie loved her new shoes, and had the feeling that her new shoes loved her back. They would never absent themselves just to reflect, and would never make occult demands on her in the bedroom.

Rosalie put her lip gloss back in her purse and pulled out a cigarette that she was quick to light.

"I just would have been really uncomfortable," she replied, releasing a cloud of smoke. "I would have had absolutely nothing to say to him."

Bénédicte winked at her.

"You could have said, 'Hi, white meat or dark?'"

Bénédicte emitted a nasal piggy laugh, rrhoinrrg! rrhoinrrg! screwing her face up so that her eyebrows, once again, disappeared into her forehead. Of course, Rosalie didn't see anything to laugh about. She smiled all the same, but just out of pity for Bénédicte, who, where hysteria was concerned, had fared much worse the night she'd split from her boyfriend, Nicolas. In April, when he got home at dawn, Bénédicte was waiting for him in the living room. He'd explained that he'd spent the evening with a client from Vancouver, and that they'd gone to talk about the Dow Jones and Nasdaq over a pizza after the bars closed. "I couldn't stop the guy, it's always three hours earlier in the Rockies, you understand?" Nicolas kept insisting it was all true until Bénédicte asked him why, in that case, there were two condoms missing from the box, pulling out a bright green giant-sized Life Styles package from behind her back, and brandishing it fiercely in his face. "You're counting rubbers now?" Nicolas shot back. He called her "pitiful and pathetic," but his face was quietly decomposing all the while. "It's Sandrine!?!" screamed Bénédicte. "The new girl in your office, eh, I know it's her!" Faced with Nicolas's silence, Bénédicte with her own two arms hoisted the oak dining-room table and sent this noble piece of woodwork, inherited from her grandfather, hurtling against the brick wall. She screamed, and her scream surprised even herself, because it seemed to emanate from her stomach rather than her throat. Nicolas called 911. A few minutes later two policemen, a man and a woman, appeared at their door. Bénédicte was crouched in a fetal position on the cool bathroom tiles. "Madame? Your partner tells us you frightened him," they declared baldly. Bénédicte tried to explain as clearly as possible the reasons for her behaviour, ending every sentence with "two condoms are missing from the box." But did that interest them really? The policewoman eyed admiringly the front-loading clothes washer in stainless steel that Bénédicte had acquired a few months earlier. Finally the police left the apartment without making a report, and the next week, Bénédicte sublet the condo of her cousin who had gone abroad to work, thus resigning herself to storing her own furniture and appliances in a gloomy warehouse in the city's southwest.

On the fourth floor of the building on the other side of Laurier, whose ground floor was occupied by a florist, a bald, bare-chested, hirsute man appeared. He leaned into space and shook his fist.

"Shut the hell up, you louts," he shouted. "People are trying to sleep! Go home! Fuck!"

He disappeared with a banging of his shutters. In the line people exchanged startled looks, discreet laughter, a few "he thinks we're the louts?" and "sicko." The doorman for B*** came down the four steps separating him from the sidewalk and made his way towards the little gang near the clay flowerpot, smoking cigarettes and exercising their lungpower.

"Federer, he's no bloody champion anymore!"

"*T'es pas sérieux*! Besides, he's sexy."

The doorman had a few words with them. He went along the line, murmuring, "*Moins fort, s'il vous plaît*. Please, keep it down!"

Then he resumed his position at the top of the stairs, and started to crack his knuckles.

"He's really myopic," sighed Bénédicte, making a face at him.

But Rosalie wasn't listening. Her eyes riveted on the shutters that had just slammed closed in the night, she was remembering an evening from the previous winter. Thierry had found her in bed with a stiff neck, mumbling her way through her prayers, trying to get to sleep and forget her pain. He'd gone to chew out the two students from the National Theatre School who lived in the apartment overhead, so they would turn down their Javanese music with its unbearable percussion. Rosalie remembered Thierry leaving her alone in the bedroom with a blistering hot Magic Bag coiled around her neck, and promising that she would get to sleep or his name wasn't Thierry

Gagnon. Just a few seconds later, the music stopped. What a relief she then felt! She waited for Thierry to come back into the bedroom to thank him, to tell him that he was her hero, her Tarzan, her Superman, but instead of coming in to check on her when he got back, he stayed in the living room and read his newspaper. And so Rosalie was lulled to sleep by the rustling of pages being turned, without being able to tell Thierry how much she appreciated what he had done for her. That is why, even now, in her moments of greatest anguish, she sometimes thought that it wasn't so much her "blockage" that drove Thierry away, but her inability to tell him how much she loved him, how good he was for her. "Perhaps he was wounded in his masculinity in the long run," she would say to Bénédicte. But her friend objected. "Stop thinking it's always your fault, Rosalie. Listen, I had *no* blockage with Nicolas, and I virtually gave him an Olympic medal every time he remembered to take out the garbage, and look at what that did for *me*!"

Two or three minutes passed, during which Rosalie and Bénédicte said nothing. Tired of waiting, half a dozen girls left the line, their high heels clattering on the pavement, and with little whoops and bursts of laughter climbed into a large taxi, earrings and bracelets tinkling. Watching the group squirming around in the vehicle, Rosalie wondered where they were going – to another bar, or, who knows, a discotheque with a sticky dance floor where they would wriggle around, drinking bad vodka offered them by boys with glazed eyes. Rosalie would have liked to know where Thierry spent his Saturday nights since he'd moved in with his brother. She wondered if he, too, missed the time when they spent their evenings cooking salmon in tinfoil on the barbecue, swimming in her sister's belowground pool in Pierrefonds, skimming along the Lachine Canal on rollerblades, or devouring *Harry Potter*, lying head to foot on the balcony hammock. As though she could read Rosalie's thoughts, Bénédicte suddenly said, "I'm really depressed!"

Rosalie came out of her daydream.

"Me too."

"You know what depresses me the most?"

"No."

"Even if Nicolas came crawling to tell me it hadn't worked out with Sandrine, even if he begged me to take him back, even if he asked me to marry him, I wouldn't want anything to do with him. I don't love him anymore."

"Isn't that good news?"

"Not at all! I feel empty. At least pain and anger fill you up."

Rosalie hesitated for a long moment before venturing, "Surely you'll... I imagine... meet someone else?"

Because one might wonder: with this new way Bénédicte had of plucking her eyebrows, would it even be possible? Rosalie wasn't sure if, as a friend, from a compassionate, detached perspective, she should talk to Bénédicte about her eyebrows. Of course, it would be to Bénédicte's benefit to know she was, as it were, disfigured. But Rosalie was afraid her friend might get angry, and as a result she would be fated – and the way things were going, this was not out of the question – to spend every Saturday night alone for the rest of her life. So she just repeated, trying to give it a little more oomph, "You'll meet someone else!"

"Yeah," agreed Bénédicte. "You too. Soon there'll be a guy, somewhere, who'll fall head over heels in love with you."

Rosalie grew sombre. "But is that what I really want? Bukowski says love dries up faster than sperm. Maybe it's better to stay lucid, even if it hurts?"

Bénédicte stuck two fingers into her mouth. "Yuk,

Bukowski! When I meet a guy who trips on Bukowski, he's always a manic depressive with greasy hair."

"That's true enough," Rosalie agreed. "They're always guys with problems."

"*Guys with problems*," Bénédicte repeated. "Isn't that a tautology?"

Rosalie smiled at this witticism before bursting out laughing, as Bénédicte was once more in the throes of her piggy chortle, rrhoinrrg! rrhoinrrg!, which was in the long run contagious. In the line, a few people whose faces were illuminated by the yellow street light turned to look at them, and the two friends exploded all the more, as though, now that peoples' eyes were on them, they wanted to keep them there. But they all turned and went back to their own conversations. Rosalie and Bénédicte caught their breath.

"Did my mascara run?" asked Rosalie.

Bénédicte assured her it had not. But Rosalie had her doubts, because her friend, while answering, instead of inspecting her lashes or the contours of her eyes, was checking out four guys who had just joined the end of the line, of which the most solidly built was none other than the Jean-Philippe who, three weeks earlier, at the very height of the most intimate moment he'd shared with her, had cried out, "Oh,

Valérie! Val!" Meanwhile, Rosalie instantly forgot the state of her makeup, and for good reason: at the bottom of the purse she was holding against her side, she felt her cell phone buzzing, which, as though by sympathetic vibration, got her jumpy as well. Who could be trying to get her at this late hour, she wondered, as her fingers with their gnawed nails pulled frantically at the zipper. Of course there weren't that many possibilities, that's why she was so fidgety, congratulating herself in her head for not having given in to the temptation of leaving a message on Thierry's voicemail last Thursday night on the pretext that she was still receiving mail in his name at the apartment and that – why not, now that you think of it, after all, it's been a while – they could go for a coffee. Because Rosalie had been reflecting, and had come to the following conclusion: better to let Thierry come back to her on his own, which shouldn't take too long. Because in the last four months it's clear he would have had time to mess about, to live the experiences he dreamed of, and he will have realized by now that the complicity he shared with Rosalie over three years was irreplaceable, and could quite easily compensate for this "blockage," which, after all – Rosalie had done her research – was the lot of forty to sixty-five percent of women, according to the Internet site she consulted. So it was Thierry on the other end of the line. He'd come back from an evening out, his mind fired up by alcohol, which takes away all your inhibitions and puts you in touch with your deepest desires, wanting to find her again, to beg for her forgiveness, her understanding, her blessing. Rosalie rummaged in her purse; she went through her lip gloss, her keys, her wallet, her blusher, her tube of lubricant for her contact lenses, as well as some old balls of Kleenex, before getting her hand on her telephone. Her ordeal was coming to an end. Good-bye to Normand the uncivilized who left her on a street corner at four o'clock in the morning! Good-bye to waiting lines, anguished lucidity, peevish tautologies! All that, really, wasn't her, and Bénédicte could easily find another partner to keep her company on these nocturnal outings to B***. Rosalie much preferred her salmon in tinfoil and her hammock, and even, if it came to that, her stiff neck.

She extracted her telephone from her purse, unfolded it, and flattened it against her ear.

"Hello?"

She was short of breath and her cheeks were crimson. Bénédicte was looking at her questioningly while fixing the clasp of her gold chain at the back of her neck. Rosalie stared wide-eyed at the sidewalk for a long few seconds.

"That'll pass," she said finally into her phone. "It's just a matter of getting used to it. But no, you're not an idiot. It's like quitting smoking. The first weeks are the hardest."

Then she stopped talking, except for the odd "umhum..." and "yes..." She hung up and shook her head. Geneviève, with whom they had eaten, was in tears. She'd not been able to sleep after they left, so she'd climbed on her bicycle in her bathrobe and had burst into the downtown restaurant where Mathieu was waiting on tables, only to find that he wasn't even working there anymore.

"One more cretin," remarked Bénédicte, stoic, then she added, dreamily, "But on your bike in a bathrobe? Phew. Takes guts."

Before returning her cell phone to her purse, Rosalie looked at the time on the lit screen. A long sigh was lodged at the bottom of her throat. It was almost one in the morning and it was as though this summer would never end.

THE APERITIF

....

It was December and there wasn't yet any snow. To mark Josiane's thirtieth birthday, Martin had reserved a suite in a Saint Paul Street hotel, in Old Montreal. The plan was the following: on the Friday they would celebrate the event in private; on Saturday, with us.

Saturday had arrived at last. At six o'clock, Carole started flitting back and forth in the apartment. She tried on dresses and asked my opinion. I sat in the living room with my bowl of sunflower seeds, my daily snack. "And this? And this?" She didn't really give me time to respond. She went back into the bedroom where, her head buried in the drawers, she cursed winter for making her wear nylon stockings, "the most uncomfortable female accessory ever invented."

"It's still practical for bank robbers," I pointed out.

Carole made a face; she's a sensitive girl. She doesn't like fabric that makes you perspire, nor fabric that itches, nor that sticks too much to the skin. Maybe it has something to do with her profession as an accountant, which favours columns of numbers that are straight, smooth, and tidy. Or maybe not. I really don't care, I stopped trying to understand a long time ago. My hands are full of damp shells, I'm going to toss them in the garbage and rinse the salt from my palms.

"And what do you think of this? Oh, you're going to spoil your appetite again with your sunflower seeds!"

I went out for some air. In the street I stumbled on a clutch of singers sporting bonnets with bells, trying to spread the Christmas spirit. I stopped for a moment and lit a cigarette. They were terribly off-key, which probably explains why the goldfish bowl in front of them was empty. My cell phone's voicemail was empty too, that gave us something in common that was not to my advantage. I hesitated a moment over the keys. They glowed in the night, little sirens ready to play me their intoxicating melody, but the evening was almost upon us, and I tucked the instrument back in my pocket. I continued my stroll, telling myself that the sirens of yesteryear had abandoned the cold ocean waters to set up residence in cell phones, whose analogue, digital, and satellite networks had taken on epic proportions. That's my poetic side; I've been to university. I went back home. During my absence, Carole had decided to wear jeans and a blouse; one must never lose hope in the human race. She wrapped Josiane's present: a grey cashmere scarf. I had to help her. There was sticky tape, tissue paper, rosettes, ribbons, it was very complicated. And that wasn't all; there was also a card. Carole had chosen one with a drawing of a thin woman straddling a motorcycle, clutching a big purple cat against her chest. Inside she had written an entire novel addressing – and I summarize – dreams, love, happiness, fulfilment, the best friend ever, equilibrium. I corrected this mawkish logorrhoea's spelling errors, and signed in the corner where there was a little room left: "Bruno xxx."

It was seven-thirty. I said, "Good, so should we go?" I was getting impatient. Carole: "Oh, yes." Full of enthusiasm I threw on my coat, but ten minutes later she was still in the bathroom. "I'm hot," I pointed out. I had planted myself in the doorway. She played with her makeup tubes for a few more minutes. I saw my reflection in the mirror and took the opportunity to neaten my hair. With my Little Prince curls, I looked quite nice. In the taxi Carole curled up against me and asked my forgiveness. Her kiss left my mouth sticky. She told me it was the honey balm for her lips and passed me a handkerchief.

Martin opened the door. A cigar at the corner of his mouth, shirt collar unbuttoned, he was being stylish. I shook his hand, and we got rid of our coats. François and Myriam were already there, parked on the leather couch, smoking cigarettes and sipping kirs. Martin asked us what we wanted as an aperitif. We took the same thing. Like an adolescent in his parents' basement, Martin had improvised a bar in a corner of the room, on an ordinary table. The ice buckets were stuffed with bottles of Bourgogne Aligoté. There was also hard liquor and syrup of cassis.

"Where's the birthday girl?" asked Carole.

That's what I wanted to know, but I was being discreet. I did the tour, looking interested, impressed even. There was a brick wall and three big windows draped in beige curtains opening onto a courtyard.

This was covered in frozen blades of grass. On the hotel's Internet site I'd seen a photo of that courtyard in the summer, with a terrace all in flower, but that was a far cry from the bleak prospect before my eyes. I'd also seen pictures of "superior suites," and Martin had not chosen the most luxurious, no matter what he claimed. I would have thought that, having been named marketing director of a doughnut company, he would at last be spending his money the way he'd always had us believe. In my opinion there's nothing worse than a braggart crossed with a miser crossed with a hawker of little industrial cakes. The ceiling was lined with wooden beams and metal pipes in which were reflected the caramel hues of the cherry-wood floors. The bed was large, too large for two, buried under a mound of cushions and white pillows. Carole was sitting on one corner. I did the same, balancing myself on the edge.

"She shouldn't be long," said Martin, serving us our kirs. "She's at the spa."

"Oh wow! A spa!" Carole cooed, placing a hand on my thigh. She'd done the same thing in the elevator five minutes earlier, when she saw the photo of a naked woman lying on her stomach, transfigured by bliss: SUBLIME SPA ON THE TENTH FLOOR WITH

SPLENDID VIEW OF THE RIVER. It was pretentious, this hotel. I wondered if Martin knew it was once a veterinary hospital for horses. For quite a while now a big fuss has been made about these boutique hotels. My colleagues in the "Style" or "Life" sections – it comes to the same thing – devote entire pages to them, but when you take a closer look they're just superannuated ruins where you can sleep for three hundred dollars a night on the spot where old nags used to be euthanized.

A syrupy bell rang. "Room service!" Two employees entered, pushing a wagon covered in plates bearing multicoloured sushis. Martin was giving them their tip, when Josiane made her appearance. Blue jogging pants, tight T-shirt, porcelain skin, oily hair, sneakers with their laces undone, this girl glowed like an electric lightbulb. She declared that they'd just anointed her body with cocoa, and excused herself to take a shower. She disappeared behind a heavy mirrored door, where Martin gave himself the once over before undoing another button at the neck of his shirt. He had a beauty mark at the corner of his lips. One day someone would have to tell him that at first glance, or when viewed from afar, it looks like a cold sore.

Myriam rubbed against me on her way to the sushi

wagon. Her crow-black hair set off her slender nape. She wore a miniskirt and a plunging neckline with the assurance of those who know they won't be able to do so for that much longer. She put the plates on the coffee table. Martin put the latest Morcheeba on the CD player, François rolled a joint, and Carole turned towards me:

"Did she really say cocoa?"

Her nostrils trembled. I kissed her, but for the wrong reasons. So she would be quiet, for instance, and to take the edge off my emotional reaction to Josiane's appearance. It didn't do much good. Carole immediately started talking about what she wanted to do for her thirtieth birthday, next April. I was subjected to her frenetic prattle concerning country inns, four-fork table settings, designer clothes, until Josiane finally came out of the bathroom in a black dress topped with naughty frills. Martin served her an aperitif while we all descended on her to give her a kiss and wish her happy birthday. When my turn came, I whispered in her ear that she should meet me in the hotel lobby, after which I announced to everybody that there were no chopsticks for the sushi. As I crossed the threshold, I heard Myriam swear that she'd seen them somewhere in paper packets. But

François told her she'd probably been pulling too hard on her joint. Martin said "As usual!" and after I don't know what because at some point the door had to close.

In the elevator I said good evening to a man and woman of about fifty, then I pulled the chopsticks out of my underpants because they were scratching me.

"Are you enjoying your stay?" I asked them.

The man smiled. He was the type who must have made a fool of himself at some point in his life as well.

"*A bit cold, but very pleasant.*"

He spoke in English; they were from Toronto.

"*Hope you don't plan to eat with those,*" the woman murmured.

She probably had a son my age. The doors opened on the ground floor, I let them go first, then I flung the chopsticks into the fireplace. They caught fire. I threw myself onto a leather loveseat, the same model as in the room, and I lit a cigarette. There must have been some of that lousy honey balm left on my lips because the filter got all sticky. I wiped my mouth on the sleeve of my sweater. Josiane came out of the elevator and walked rapidly in my direction. That girl was so beautiful that she could have been a model or an actress. Instead, she's a researcher for a radio program. Something dumb for consumers, where the host tells you whether leeks will cost less than radishes this week.

"You've got three minutes!" she barked. "I said I'd forgotten my wallet at the spa."

I asked her to sit beside me. I didn't know where to start. I'm always afraid for my diction in front of this girl, of not knowing how to put two words together. She took a puff of my cigarette and I slipped a hand into her damp hair.

"Listen, Josi, dammit. I know we said we'd stop, but it's hard. I'm always thinking about you."

She leaned back in the loveseat and crossed her legs. She looked at the fire. The chopsticks were just a pile of ash.

"Me too, Bruno, I think of you."

It's very complicated between us. For the moment she allowed me to caress the back of her neck, her hair and face, even if some of the hotel employees must have seen her with Martin since their arrival yesterday. Josiane likes taking risks, but they're always calculated. The first afternoon we found ourselves together it was at her place, in Martin's absence; he never gets home before six o'clock, preoccupied as he is with the fate of his doughnuts. Josiane waited until five o'clock before throwing me out. One day when I was in particularly good form, we stretched it out to five-thirty. We'd been going along like that since early fall, until Josiane let me know, two weeks previous, that she didn't know where she was at anymore. Stupid. Just looking at her, I could almost sense the beating of her heart behind her eyes. I knew she had regrets. My cell phone rang.

"White House, can I help you?"

"Are you still in the restaurant?"

It was Carole.

"Yes."

"Can you bring back three or four bottles of Perrier?"

I said yes and hung up. I turned back towards Josiane and plunged my gaze into hers. She told me to stop looking at her like that, but how is a man supposed to look at a woman who won't let him sleep, for whom he would like to become a botanist to create a rose of the same blue as her eyes, for whom he'd spend his Sundays making soup instead of watching football? Josiane observed that I didn't even know how to open a can, and I said okay, so I'm getting carried away, it was just an example. I changed the subject.

"What's this business about cocoa?"

"I don't know. It seems that it penetrates your pores and gives you energy."

I asked her if it works. She shrugged her shoulders and buried her face in my neck. Her breath made a little breeze in my hair, this girl is sensual even in distress. Her eyelashes tickled me, but I tried hard not to squirm, because that wouldn't be very masculine. Never before had there been a question of my leaving Carole, nor of her leaving Martin. Perhaps the time had come to float the idea? As soon as the words were out of my mouth, I felt her stiffen in my arms. "Are you crazy?" she exclaimed. She went on that she was fine with Martin, that she didn't want to turn her life upside down. Suddenly, I thought of that thin woman straddling a motorcycle and holding her big cat against her chest, and it occurred to me that we were like that. It was clear that symbolically, in the second degree, I was the motorcycle and Martin was the cat. My telephone rang again.

"James Bond?"

"Are you still in the restaurant?"

It was Myriam.

"What do you want?"

"I prefer San Pellegrino. The bubbles are smaller."

"Ten-four."

I was starting to hang up when she murmured, "I want to talk to you tonight."

"You think this is a good time?"

Josiane's phone rang now and made a real racket. She got up and went to answer a little way off, behind a chubby Christmas tree whose branches were weighed down with lights, stars, little angels, and candy canes.

"I've had enough," Myriam was erupting on the other end of the line. "You've been telling me that for three months."

I told her to calm down if she didn't want to spoil the evening. She informed me that she was locked in the bathroom with her third kir, away from the others, who were on their fourth. She described the Jacuzzi and the multiheaded shower. I suspected she had something dirty in mind. I interrupted.

"My batteries are dead."

"Don't move, I'm coming down!"

"No!"

I hung up. Josiane was on her way back.

"Martin found my wallet on the night table. I have to go up."

"You should have brought it with you, Josi!"

She called the elevator and crossed her arms over her chest. She said she didn't know anymore where she was. She reproached me for my stubbornness and accused me of making the situation even more difficult.

"It's my birthday, dammit."

She smiled at me sadly as the elevator doors shut me off from her. I thought, love hurts, love drives you crazy, and then, in the end, it lets you down. I could play the starring role in a sad song. I flicked my finger at an angel face hanging from the tree. In the restaurant, they wanted to seat me. "Smoking or non-smoking?" The lighting was dim and the clientele sparse. I went to the bar, where I ordered four bottles of Perrier, a bottle of San Pellegrino, six pairs of chopsticks for sushi, and a kir, why not? The couple I'd run into in the elevator was at one of the tables. The woman was studying her menu, while toying with her pearl necklace. The man was going through the leather-bound wine list with a fine-tooth comb. I made my decision; tonight I would be a hero. I would leave them all. I would shake off the chains that were binding me, I would embrace peace, serenity, and freedom. Yes, I'd made up my mind. "Forty-three dollars," said the girl behind the bar. I felt like answering "Room 505," and signing the bill Martin Desrochers. Doubtless my salary as a journalist writing about dogs hit by cars couldn't match his, but I had my pride. I paid cash. Myriam climbed onto the stool next to mine. Her miniskirt rode up to reveal her well-rounded thighs.

"I said I'd forgotten my cell phone in the car. Why do you run away from me all the time?"

There are people to whom you have to repeat everything three times over. For Myriam, you can multiply that by four, because she always thinks she's right. So I got on with it. I launched the cassette. Like every other time we've found ourselves together since the end of summer, I explained I couldn't go on lying to Carole. I had made my choice: it was with her that I wanted to spend the rest of my life. To align myself, to better myself, to reproduce myself, and all the rest. Without taking her eyes off me Myriam gulped down some of my kir, batted her eyelashes, curled her upper lip. She assumed her role of the hangdog child-woman. Thanks to her studies in psychology, this girl has managed to hone her manipulative techniques to a fare-thee-well. She used to spend her days making the rounds of the city's jails to lend an ear to the in-mates' confessions. She has a weakness for hooligans, that's clear, and sometimes I wonder if that's why she has trouble letting go of me, but she's going to have to find a way. I try to encourage it: Frank is a neat guy. He takes care of her. He's in the same line of work. Common interests are very important, you know, my dear. When we'll be seventy years old, aside from our pensions, that's all we'll have left to share, or almost.

"Don't tell me what I should do. It's with you I feel good, I'm fed up with spilling my guts every three days into your cell phone's voicemail."

Just then it rang.

"Speak of the devil."

"I thought your batteries were dead!"

I slapped a finger to her lips.

"The Pentagon, hello."

"We're starving to death, what are you up to?"

It was Martin. I told him I was on my way but I'd forgotten the room number. He'd forgotten it too. Myriam drew my finger into her mouth and nibbled it, sucked it, gnawed it, slurped it, chewed on it. Carole took the phone.

"Alzheimer! It's 505. Hurry up!"

I hung up.

"Give me back my finger."

Myriam calmly shook her head. She didn't let go. Her palate and her tongue were pulling mightily on my index finger. She was really going at it, the little animal, she likes that. When she spat it out, it was bright red and dripping saliva. I wiped it on my jeans.

Myriam jumped up from her stool and took the six packages of chopsticks, I took the five bottles of water, and we ran for the suite. In the elevator I backed her against the wall and thrust my tongue into her mouth. The rounded derrière of the girl being sublimely pampered at the spa was right in my face. I got an erection. At the fourth floor, Myriam squirmed and started to sigh. The elevator stopped at the fifth, I told her to carry on to the eighth so we wouldn't get back to the room at the same time. She called me a son of a bitch and shoved the chopsticks into my mouth. I couldn't reply.

A scent of eucalyptus was hanging in the hallway. In front of Room 505, I closed my eyes and waited. I thought of things that would get my erection down. Of singers with bells on their hats. Of the city of Toronto. Back in the room, I spat the chopsticks onto the bed.

"Did you go to get them in China?" Carole piped up.

"You mean Japan, my sweet."

"I hope you put the bottles on our room," Martin bellowed.

"That's my affair," I said.

Myriam came in two minutes later.

"Did you find it?" asked François.

"Between two chairs," she answered, brandishing the phone.

The bottles of Bourgogne Aligoté were propped upside down in the ice buckets. Martin spilled them into a bag and replaced them with bottles of Chardonnay. My kir was still there on the bedside table. It was lukewarm, but I finished it anyway. Josiane was in the bathroom rinsing the glasses we'd used for the aperitifs, as there weren't enough for the meal. Martin had had an accident, Carole told me, as she applied another layer of honey balm to her lips. He'd wanted to light the candles on the table, but he'd brushed the glasses with his unbuttoned shirt sleeve. Result: three glasses less.

"But what's wrong with your finger?" she suddenly exclaimed.

My index finger had not yet recovered from Myriam's assault. It even seemed a bit more purple. I stared at it, stupefied. Out of the corner of my eye, I saw Myriam coolly pulling on her cigarette, while François tilted his head back and put fresh drops in his eyes. Martin was looking for another CD to play. I frowned. On the spur of the moment I said, "I hope it's not the sunflower seeds."

Carole pouted disapprovingly.

"Did you go back to that bulk store?"

Since she had found a nail clipping large enough for a big toe in the dried cranberries, we'd vowed to boycott that cut-rate establishment in our neighbourhood. A promise I've never broken, as a matter of fact.

"I keep telling you to go to the fruit store!"

I frowned again. I was very nervous.

"You think it might be a tropical parasite, or what?"

As she did not put the lie to my suspicions, I announced that I was going in search of a disinfectant. In the bathroom, Josiane was drying the wineglasses with toilet paper. I remarked that she was a very mediocre housekeeper. She asked me what I wanted. "Some ointment," I said, showing her my finger. She recoiled, then put down the glass and took my hand in hers.

"But what's that?"

I sighed.

"What do you think? It's a rash. It's a nervous reaction. You see how you're driving me crazy?"

She glanced at the half-open door. Her dress strap slipped off her shoulder. I put it back in place and caressed her cheek with my healthy hand. She let my mouth brush hers. Then I read on her lips: "Wednesday." She went out with the three poorly washed glasses after slipping me a tube of moisturizing cream. I put a little on my finger, and then something very strange happened. For a moment I thought I'd developed a rash due to stress from being disappointed in love. But I immediately remembered that I'd caught a parasite in a bag of sticky seeds, a poisonous worm or a pathogenic bacteria. It took me several seconds, a long time, to recall Myriam's cavernous mouth. And then I had to grip the counter, all these layered lies were making me dizzy, they were fragmenting my consciousness. The others were calling me, they were chanting that they were hungry. I pulled myself together. I splashed cold water on my face, dabbed at myself with a towel, and with no more ado, I went to join them.

WILDERNESS LAKE

The others were getting ready for the Saturday night party. They decorated the common room with multi-coloured banners, put bowls of chips on the tables, tested the microphone, "one two, one two," and picked CDs out of the big box. When all the counsellors had their backs turned, I raised my thumb in the air for Flavie, that was the signal we had agreed upon, and Annie and I took off, walking at first, then running once we got to the stairs. We got through the door, no one in sight, crossed the parking lot, and took the little road.

"You're going to do the talking," Annie said. "When you talk, Mama can't say no to her little baby."

I told Annie that I wasn't a little baby anymore, and I started singing to rehearse the number Flavie and I were performing at the Saturday night party: "*If you want my love, nananana... For me, nana... ha!*"

I didn't know all the words by heart, but it didn't matter. Flavie had decided we could fall back on our dance steps.

"Walk quicker," Annie said.

We'd been at the summer camp for two weeks and we were leaving the next day, but Annie didn't want to think about that because she was in love with Gabriel, a boy in the Mushroom group who spent all season here. That morning my sister had told me about her plan; we would wait for the right time, then in secret we'd go to the phone booth just off the highway. The day before, Annie had asked her counsellor, Butterfly, if she could use the phone in the office, but Butterfly told her it was forbidden for campers to call anybody unless it was urgent. Annie hadn't pushed her luck. She didn't like Butterfly because the week before she'd made her go climbing, and Annie has vertigo; she doesn't even go out on the balcony when she visits my uncle Henri who lives on the fifth floor. Anyway, if Mama gave us permission to stay, she'd only have to phone the camp owner herself to tell her she could keep us another week, but no longer, because after that Papa would be taking us to the seashore.

The little road we were following was gravel. It was lined with bushes, maples, and birches. Birches are my favourite trees because they have no bark, just a very thin skin, white or beige, sometimes almost pink. Since my arrival at the summer camp, I'd started a collection of birch skins. I'd pull gently on the little dry ends that make curls on the trunks, and peel them off. Sometimes the pieces of skin could be really big, they could stretch almost all the way around the tree. Flavie said it wasn't nice to do that to the trees because it must hurt them. She knew how many skins I'd collected because, to flatten them, I'd put them under my mattress, and Flavie slept in the bed just below mine. To defend myself I'd explained that birch skin grows back really fast, but I wasn't sure if this was true.

Annie walked faster than I did, and I had trouble keeping up.

"Wait for me!"

Annie said we had no time to lose.

At first my sister didn't even want to come here. One night when we were doing our homework in the kitchen, Mama stuck a brochure on the refrigerator door with photos of children playing in the water, and said, "Look, that's where you're going this summer, girls." As though she'd not heard a thing, Annie said, "Mama, when was the French Revolution?" To copy her, I recited my lesson out loud: "The porpoise is a marine mammal." Mama got angry: "You're not happy?" Annie said no, and the next days she sulked, because she thought it would be like a daycare. One morning, she ripped the brochure off the refrigerator door, and we tore it up together. "Mama won't find the address," Annie said, but in the end she didn't even need it because she just dropped us off in a shopping-centre parking lot and a yellow bus took us to the camp.

Now that Annie wanted to stay longer, I pretended that I was in favour of it too, but I didn't care if we went back the next day. I was eager to put all my birch skins into an album, and I'd had enough of sleeping in a bunkbed; I was afraid of falling down in my sleep. Besides, in the cafeteria, Dolorès, the lady who took care of our nutrition, made hot chocolate with water, not even with milk. Once, the expiry date for my yogurt was three days overdue. I told her so she would give me another one, but she said I should eat it because all the Third World children were dying of hunger, as though I didn't already know. Finally I went back to my seat with the yogurt and gave it to Flavie.

Maybe I would have wanted to stay here longer too, if I'd succeeded in drowning myself in the lake so that Wapiti my beautiful counsellor would do mouth to mouth on me and fall madly in love. But my plan never worked. Every time we went out in a canoe we had to wear a life vest, and Tarantula, the other counsellor, gave us hell if she saw it wasn't zipped right to the chin. The only times we didn't have to wear it was when they let us go swimming where it was shallow, but I never went because Jasmin, who comes here every year, told me a girl had vomited blood for four days two summers ago because she'd been attacked by a poisonous bloodsucker hiding in the sand.

When we went out in the canoe, Jasmin was my partner. He let me sit in the canoe near the lawn and he pushed it into the lake, that way I didn't have to walk in the wet sand and risk being bitten by a blood-sucker. He ran the danger for me. I might have wanted to stay longer if Jasmin hadn't left, but at the beginning of the week, during a nature study on the mountain, he was stung by a bee. He swelled all up and Tarantula had to run with him in her arms to the infirmary. That night someone from his family came to get him, and after that I never heard anything more. I hope he got better.

Annie tied her ponytail high up on her head. She said that if Mama didn't let her stay longer, she'd never see Gabriel again in her whole life because he lived at the end of the world, farther even than Grandpa, and Grandpa, it took an hour in the car to go and visit him in the home where he played cards with the other old men. In the end Grandpa peed in his pyjamas, and now he's dead. Mama says he's still there somewhere, like a guardian angel among us; it seems we can even talk to him, but I haven't tried, for me it's much too scary.

I stopped to pick some raspberries in the bushes and ran to catch up with Annie.

"You want some?"

She said she wasn't hungry, so I swallowed them all. Then I wiped my hands full of raspberry juice on my pants and decided that I'd never have enough clean clothes to get through another week.

"If someone sees we're gone, what's she going to say, your friend Flavie?"

It was a good question. I'd told Flavie to cover for us if the counsellors came looking, but I wasn't sure that was such a good idea because she'd never come up with a good lie. Flavie wasn't that bright, which is why I had no problem slipping her my rotten yogurt the other morning; I knew she wouldn't notice. The only thing Flavie cares about is her hair. That's what got us talking in the first place. We'd just arrived and were settling into the dormitory. Flavie had the bed under mine. I was unrolling my sleeping bag when she climbed on my ladder. "Do you want to brush my hair? It's all tangled because of the wind on the bus." I got down and she handed me the brush. I sat on her bed and she got on her knees with her back turned. There were lots of knots in her long black hair. So I pulled hard. Flavie started to scream. She explained: "You've got to go knot by knot, and hold up each piece of hair before brushing." It took me fifteen minutes to do her whole head. I noticed that she'd painted her toenails, and I decided she was an airhead, but she became my friend anyway because the other girls were even worse than she was.

After Jasmin left, Flavie agreed to push the canoe into the lake so my feet wouldn't touch the sand. The problem is that she doesn't push as fast as Jasmin, and the canoe almost always tips over before even entering the water. Flavie gets mad to make me get out of the canoe to help her, but all I have to say is that I won't brush her hair anymore and she starts pushing again. Apparently she has a whole collection of hair elastics at home, but she didn't bring them with her to the camp because she was afraid the little coloured balls and the other decorations would break. So that we'd stay friends after camp was over, she said she'd send me the elastics she has two of in the mail. I can't give her any of my birch skins because they're all different.

I looked at the sky. A lot of the time clouds look like things I know: animals, objects, people, but now they didn't make me think of anything. They were just clouds, because I was trying to follow Annie, and she was walking too fast for me to be able to look at them closely.

"Get a move on, Véro."

We couldn't yet see the highway ahead of us, and behind us the camp had disappeared. I went close to the trees to see if there was any interesting birch skin on the trunks, but I heard a strange noise, like someone coughing. I ran back and squeezed myself up against my sister.

"Did you hear?"

"What?"

Except for heights, Annie's never afraid of anything.

The Saturday before, my group, the Bulrushes,

went on the exercise course. We had to climb rope walls, walk on shaky wooden bridges, crawl through cement pipes, and do even harder things. I wasn't good at it and besides found it boring, so I asked Flavie if she wanted to cut through the woods and meet up with the others where the course ended. That would give me time to gather more birch skins. We were going out of the clearing into the woods when a man came out from behind a thick tree trunk. He lowered his pants and showed us his thing. Flavie cried out really loud and Wapiti came running, but not fast enough because the man and his thing had disappeared into the forest. Flavie threw herself into Wapiti's arms without even leaving any room for me. Everyone stopped exercising and went back to the camp. The owner called the police. Flavie was crying because she wanted to phone her mother, but she couldn't because her mother was on a cruise with her new husband. When the police arrived, they showed us drawings of all sorts of men's faces and asked us if it was one of them that we'd seen in the forest. Flavie kept crying and didn't say anything, and me neither because it wasn't the man's head I'd seen, but his thing.

That night Annie got back from her canoe camping trip with her group the Marshmallows, and I told her the story while we were eating Dolorès' shepherd's pie.

She got worried. "You didn't call the parents I hope? They'd come to get us right away if they knew that." She told me she didn't want to leave anymore because she liked Gabriel. "We almost kissed behind the tent." She showed him to me at the other end of the cafeteria. He wasn't even handsome. You could see his big pointed ears sticking out from twenty metres away. I told her, "Nini, he has Spock's ears!" She looked for a few seconds, and then turned to me: "You're super dumb, his ears are fine, you're dumb."

I don't like it when my sister calls me dumb. So to scare her I told her I'd call Papa and say we couldn't stay here a minute more, that the place was super dangerous, that there was a poison bloodsucker in the lake and a man with no underpants in the woods. Annie begged me not to do that, then said she was sorry three times, and offered me her rice pudding, but I didn't want it because it smelled funny.

The gravel on the road had become asphalt and we could see the highway.

"I think I'll do the talking after all," said Annie. "You never know what you might say."

Annie was very preoccupied with her idea. We were getting near the telephone booth. We'd often passed it when the yellow bus took us to activities

outside the camp, like horseback riding. There was
no car on the horizon. Annie pushed the folding
doors and I followed her inside. We stood there for a
few seconds in front of the telephone, crammed in
like sardines. There was a scrunched-up chocolate-
bar wrapping on the shelf. Annie picked up the
receiver and pressed zero. She dictated our number
into the phone and gave our names. She jumped up
and down and chewed her nails, something Papa always told her not to do.

"This has to work," she repeated at least ten times.

All of a sudden she went stiff, and after a few seconds of silence, she said, "Hello, Mama?" in a really
sweet voice. I was too squished, so I went out of the
booth to wait for Annie by the side of the road. A big
truck went by. When he saw me, the driver went toot!
toot! and I waved back.

Inside the booth, Annie was jumping again. Her
ponytail wouldn't stay in place. The only time I'd seen
Annie so excited about getting permission was when
a neighbour's cat had babies and she wanted one.
She'd begged Mama at dinnertime "I want a little
kitty." Mama had said yes. Annie called the cat Bushy
because even if it was small it had really long hair. I
guess its hair would have grown even longer, but five

days after we adopted it, Bushy was dead. The vet said its heart was not the right shape. We dug a little hole in the yard and put Bushy in. We were getting used to it, we'd done the same thing with Grandpa, only that was at the cemetery.

I couldn't hear what Annie was saying, but she was crying into the telephone and she hung up so hard that the chocolate wrapper fell on the ground. She looked at me through the glass. Her face was red with anger and she was trying so hard not to let the tears come out of her eyes that her chin was trembling. She left the telephone booth and we went back along the little silent road lined with trees. Annie didn't walk as fast as on the way down, maybe because she was crying. I said she should breathe deeply. That's what Wapiti had told me to do when I fell off my stilts. Annie tried, but it didn't work. I stroked her cheek; if it hadn't been so wet, her skin would have been almost as smooth as that of a birch.

"We have to leave tomorrow," said Annie, hiccupping.

I held her hand in mine, loosely at first, but much tighter when, down the middle of the road, we saw two furious counsellors running in our direction.

SENTIMENTAL RISKS

Louis volunteered to go with me to the dentist, even though I hadn't asked. That was exciting. Richard, my ex, even balked at going with me to the grocery store. But I don't want to make comparisons.

In the waiting room, Louis took off his leather jacket and let it drop onto the loveseat flanked by two plastic ficuses. I leaned over the reception desk.

"Hello. I have an appointment with Doctor Giguère. Karine Simard."

The lady on the other side had grey hair with mauve highlights and brown spots on her face. She tapped at her computer's keyboard before putting her glasses back on her nose.

"Are you still on Saint Dominique?"

"Yes."

"Same phone number?

"Yes."

"We still contact Marlène in case of emergency?"

Marlène is my best friend. I glanced towards Louis. He'd begun to read a magazine. I had my eyes on him when the answer came out of my mouth.

"No."

"No?" repeated the receptionist.

Louis raised his head; I smiled at him and looked back at the woman.

"She's moved."

That was true. Last summer, Marlène piled all her possessions into a truck and unloaded them into Brian's condo. Lucky her. Out of the corner of my eye, I saw Louis resume his reading. I leaned further over the counter.

"Can you put the name Louis instead?"

I was thrown off balance at having expressed my wish as a question. Why should I need permission from this stranger? But the lady didn't take any notice; she went on poking at her keyboard while I dictated the telephone number. Through the plate-glass window behind her, downtown Montreal was going about its business. The April sky was cloudy, but the horizon line stretched out to the river. Scalloped slabs of ice glided on the water. It was romantic.

"You can go and sit down. Doctor Giguère will come and get you."

Louis was leafing through a *Golf Digest*. I grabbed a dog-eared *Chatelaine* and slumped down beside him. I put a hand on his thigh and whimpered that I had a horror of needles; he said he needed a new putter. With Louis, I feel like I'm under a glass bell, sheltered from all foreign bodies, but that didn't stop me from aiming a kindly glance at the old man smoothing the rim of his hat near the aquarium. I imagined he was a widower and could use it. The dentist called me in.

Two days later, I told Louis the news that had shaken up everyone at the bank: the young Romanian waitress at the Café Suprème in the building's lobby had posted a complaint against our director of marketing for sexual harassment. No one had seen the likes of it. He interrupted me.

"Karine, I have to tell you something."

Personally, if one day I were to write a book on the art of conversation, I would disallow this way of breaking the ice. It's a sure sign that serious matters are to follow and it can only sow panic in the individual being addressed. I put down my fork. "Of course." *His goddam ex is back on the scene. His company has gone bankrupt.* Threats like that assume forms beyond imagining.

"I'm afraid you're starting to feel too comfortable in our relationship."

We were in a restaurant, which was a good thing. Public spaces were doubtless invented so that people might stifle their urge to scream when their better halves start spouting idiocies. Because how can you reproach someone for seeking comfort? You only have to stroll through the aisles of a furniture store to see people solemnly bouncing their behinds on every couch in sight, in search of the softest. A slice of cucumber was having a hard time making it down my throat. I pinched a piece of lettuce between my thumb and my index finger, and asked Louis to elaborate. Chewing away at his trout rillettes, he explained that he'd lately observed – "but maybe I'm wrong," he added, with an air of not really believing it – that I was going too fast.

I licked my greasy fingers.

"Too fast?"

"We shouldn't cut corners," he said.

My gaze wandered in the direction of the dining room. A woman was winding her creamed pasta around her fork. Like a child, a man was cutting his steak into little pieces. A waitress was scrutinizing her nails near the bar. But the subdued lighting lent a pink complexion and sparkling eyes to everyone.

I swallowed some wine.

"I thought you were happy with me."

"Why do you always look at things negatively? I *am* happy with you. But I don't want to feel the pressure of a future all planned out in advance."

A busboy placed a candle in the centre of our table, near the bread basket. That seemed well timed. I stared at the flame until I was a little bit blinded.

"You think I'm putting pressure on you?"

"You gave my name to your dentist as a reference in case of emergency."

Looking back at Louis, I blinked my eyes.

"That was just a formality."

"But how many times a year do you go to the dentist?"

"Once."

He held his two hands out in front of him, palms up, as though to signal that he'd made his case.

"So you see what I mean? That puts pressure on me. The pressure of knowing that you think we'll still be together in a year."

Louis' hands are somewhat the worse for wear; the

skin is red, or dry, and blistered here and there. I've already given him a tube of shea butter revitalizing cream, but I found it congealed in the glove compartment of his truck. I was dumbstruck. "We won't be together in a year?"

"Perhaps. I really hope so, in fact. But for you it's like it's written in the sky, as if all that were already decided."

When the waitress came to clear the first course off our table, I was so distraught that I felt like grabbing her wrist to ask her what she thought about all that; he *hoped* we'd still be together, but he refused to envisage such an eventuality in advance. Finally, I waited for her to move off and mumbled that I would call the dentist the next morning to change the emergency number in my file. Louis left for a few minutes, to go to the bathroom. I poured myself a glass of wine, and did some self-examination. Was it true that I'd decided everything in advance? I had to admit that, for the last while, I'd been nursing a highly figurative theory. I liked to think that once past the mark of twelve, or let's say fourteen weeks, a relationship was like a fetus: the probability of abortion diminished significantly. This was a cockeyed idea and I don't know where I got it. Maybe it was because I was thirty-three years old and I sometimes wondered if my uterus would one day fulfil its intended function. That would be logical, but I still had to stop thinking in pictures.

Later, Louis told me that he'd discovered some newspapers dating back to the 1920s in the walls of the kitchen he was renovating in Verdun. He saw that I hadn't yet touched my plate. He got worried.

"Isn't it good?"

I continued pushing my food around with the end of my fork. I dug a hole in the potato purée. I pouted. I sighed. I had to get things straight.

"Do I still excite you?"

Louis rolled his eyes and softly stroked my forearm with his rough hand.

"Karine, you're super hot. Go on, eat."

I attacked my cod.

"You *cannot* go along with an attitude like that," Marlène told me the next morning.

Some of my colleagues take cigarette breaks; I take pee breaks with my cell phone. In the hallway behind the elevators there's a private bathroom. The door locks. I can talk at my leisure. The garbage is not emptied every day, so sometimes I see signs that I'm not the only one seeking a bit of privacy in that spot. Once there was a pregnancy test that had come out negative; another time, a printed e-mail torn into tiny pieces. But now the garbage can was empty. There was, however, an unpleasant odour in the air; clearly, someone had emptied their bowels not long before. My nose in the sleeve of my blouse, I punched in Marlène:

"But what do you want me to do?"

"Make a scene."

"You think?"

"Set your own limits."

"How?"

"Do I have to teach you how to read between the lines? What his argument means is that he's unsure about something. The two of you, you, the future. No?"

I saw my face growing longer in the mirror. Marlène repeated her question:

"No?"

"That's why I'm freaking out!"

"Make him choose."

"How?"

"Tell him he has to get with it. You've been together five months, you have the right to demand something stable. You *deserve* something stable,

Karine. Everybody knows that anxiety leads to cancer. That's the bottom line."

Cancer? I wondered if I was letting the matter get out of hand.

"He hasn't said he wants to slow things down with me."

"No, but he made it *very* clear that he doesn't want them to accelerate. Don't make excuses for him, you did that for three years with Richard, and look what happened there. A relationship has to evolve. It can't just stagnate. You have to tell him you want a more serious commitment on his part. Tell him it's that or nothing. After, let him stew in his own juice. He'll budge. If not, too bad."

I saw Louis trapped in a jar of beets like my grandmother used to prepare every summer at her cottage, and it gave me the willies.

"Isn't that kind of fascist?"

"If he's ready to let you drop because he doesn't really want to commit, what's there for you to lose?"

Someone was knocking on the bathroom door. I told Marlène I was seeing Louis that weekend, and I was going to think things over in the meantime. Because she must be right; how can I conceive of making headway with a man if he won't even leave a trace of himself on my dentist's computer? On paper, that looks bad.

"I've got to go."

"Do it, Karine. It's worth the risk. Nothing ventured, nothing gained. Take heart!"

I opened the door and found myself face to face with Sébastien Charbonneau, a translator I'd got into the habit of sleeping with after Happy Hour last year even though I knew he was doing the same thing with an administrative assistant.

"Hi, Karine," he said. "What's up?"

"Nothing."

He wrinkled his nose and stuck out his tongue.

"Fuck me! There's been some action in here."

Sébastien Charbonneau has a deviant nature. That's why I put an end to our little adventure.

"Don't get excited. I'm not the shitter."

"That's unfortunate."

"Excuse me."

I stuck my phone back in my jacket pocket and turned on my heels.

Was I ready to take the risk? Faced with the unknown or with serious existential questions, some people consult their horoscope. Or – as in the case of my colleague Geneviève six months ago when they discovered precancerous cells in her cervix – a psychic. Me, I dig deep into semantics. After having scoured the entire floor looking for the *Petit Robert*, griping that it's not for nothing that we're a generation of illiterates when there's just one dictionary for thirty employees in the Communications Department, I arrived at this:

Risk: The act of exposing oneself to danger (in the hope of obtaining an advantage).

To take a risk: To attempt something daring, with no guarantee as to the result.

That night, at home, I surfed the Internet, where I found a site explaining that a risk is "a potential loss, identified and quantifiable," and in this sense is to be distinguished from uncertainty, which is not quantifiable. It's true that if there's one thing I can't stand in life it's doubt and indecision. I want a pilot on the plane. Not to know where you're going is extremely irritating. If Louis refused to foresee a future with me, it's because he was uncertain of us both. But when would he be sure? Was I going to have to wait three months, a year, four years? If uncertainty is not quantifiable, maybe it's infinite. That thought really gave me a chill. I went to shut the window. The deserted street gave off a scent of spring that was fresh and moist.

Louis and I have our habits. We brush our nails in the shower. We don't forget our reusable cloth bags when we go shopping. We browse at Renaud-Bray, him in the graphic novel section, me in the magazines, we lose track of each other and call on our cell phones to arrange to meet at the cash. And we have our Saturdays, which really begin Friday nights, when I leave my three and a half in the neighbourhood of Villeray with my clothes over my shoulder to go to his place in the neighbourhood of Rosemont. In the morning, he lets me sleep while he goes to buy two croissants and a chocolatine. Then he stops at the corner store where he buys *La Presse* and a 250-millilitre carton of 1% milk for my coffee – he prefers his coffee black and never puts milk into anything, not even a drop into his cereal. For reasons known only to himself, he prefers to eat it with a kind of Lebanese yogurt whose texture is very thick and whose odour is so powerful that it never fails to elicit from me comments such as: "Did you check the expiration date?"

This Saturday when I got up Louis was reading the

"Hearth and Home" section of the paper, with his coffee in front of him. On the table, in a little wicker basket, was my croissant and my half-chocolatine, and just beside, the jar of strawberry jam. Everything was like usual, except inside my head.

"Hel-lo," I said.

His hand brushed my behind over my nightie. "Sleep well?"

I sat on his knees and the paper got crumpled between our bellies. I had to talk to him this morning. The night before, I didn't know how. Not only did the DVD of *The Departed* keep us on the edge of our seats, but we had ordered Tonkinese soup and imperial rolls from *Pékin Délices*, and besides all that we'd made love three times and I'd come five. I should make it clear that I'm not in the habit of keeping such a meticulous record of our lovemaking and its effect on me, that would be absurd. But last night, given my sensitivity to this entire situation, I did so.

Louis complained that I was crushing him. I pretended not to hear him. My head buried in his lukewarm neck, I breathed deeply. Why did he have to smell so good the morning I was going to make a scene? It was cruel. He pushed me away and dropped the paper onto the table. I asked: "Have they printed your ad?"

I slid onto the chair nearby. He said, "It's for next week."

His hair was damp, plastered onto his head in little rolls, like the fur on a wet dog's back.

"You took your shower?"

"Yes. Why?"

Did he guess I was asking stupid questions just as a diversion? Maybe nothing was the same anymore for him either. Maybe that explained his previous night's superhuman ardour. Yes, that was it, it was clear as day: Louis had channelled his anxiety into his penis. He was on fire all right, burning to know whether I had in fact called my dentist to change the emergency number in my file, which I had not.

"No reason. I didn't hear anything."

"You want your coffee?"

"Good idea!"

Louis' espresso machine was Italian and sophisticated, with its constellation of luminous buttons. A few weeks into our relationship I wanted to assert my independence and prepare my own coffee, but nothing flowed into my cup; only the built-in grinder overheated, making an infernal din. Louis was doing the washing in the basement, and I hurtled down the stairs: "Louis! Louis! I just touched the orange button and it made a noise like a steam engine!" A torrent of fabric softener poured into the washing machine's gut. "Fuck!" he exclaimed, hurling himself into the kitchen where the espresso machine was now silent and still. "But I'm telling you it was spitting smoke!" I insisted, before advising him to program two or three extra rinse cycles into the washer if he didn't want his clothes to give him a rash. "It's you who'll give me a rash if you screw up like that again," he replied, which so unsettled me that I burst into tears. Along with the time his ex phoned at one in the morning so he'd go and kill a spider in the bathroom, and I'd bellowed, "Is she retarded, or what?" and he'd explained that she was very, very phobic, and I'd answered that she just had to try hypnosis or buy herself a can of Raid, it was one of our worst episodes. In short, since then I've never touched that infernal coffee machine, and Louis has never offered to give me a lesson on how it works.

"Is it cold out?"

"Not bad."

Louis busied himself with the coffee machine, pressed the right buttons, wiped some drops of orange juice off the counter with a J-cloth, and dried his calloused hands on his cotton sweater. I thought about what Marlène had said: "What's there for you to lose?" Sure, now that she's settled into Brian's condo, Marlène can say what she likes. But if, at the start of her affair with her boss, she'd acted as radically as she wants me to do with Louis, she'd still be knocking back gin and tonics while listening to Serge Gainsbourg in her two and a half in the McGill Ghetto, and chewing out her beer-drinking neighbours for playing Arcade Fire to wake the dead. While after only five months with me, Louis was religiously making me café au lait every Saturday morning, all Brian did was take her to a hotel in Boucherville once every ten days, leaving my friend more than enough downtime to re-solve, after each of these escapades, that it would be the last. "No way I'm going to play second fiddle!" she raged. "The next time he tries it, he'll see what I'm made of!" But Marlène never had the courage to act on her threats, and getting up to press my nose against the French window, I wondered whether, in giving me such strict advice, she wanted to compensate for her own weakness in waiting more than two years now to have Brian all to herself.

In the deserted alleyway a garbage-can lid was being swept along by a gust of wind.

"Here," said Louis, handing me my bowl of coffee.

I thanked him and he went back to studying his "Hearth and Home" section of the paper. I trailed my sock feet along the floor's beige tiles, and dipped a finger into the coffee bowl. The liquid was boiling hot. I sucked at the ball of milky foam stuck to my index finger, I sat back down, and thought back on my very first meeting with Louis: it seemed so far away and strange. My mother was organizing an evening to celebrate my father's retirement, and I had arrived in the middle of the afternoon to help her with the food, to choose the music, and to arrange the living room so that the guests could circulate more easily. I was struggling to push the heavy couch against the wall when Louis burst into the room wearing camouflage pants, an old pink Vuarnet T-shirt, and a Sico cap. "Need some help?" he asked right off, and without waiting for an answer, in one movement, he shoved the piece of furniture under the window. Impressed, I nuzzled with the tip of my ballet slipper one of the four little depressions in the carpet left by the couch's legs. It was a dark green carpet that my parents had brought back from a trip to Egypt. "It's you who's renovating the kitchen in the second-floor apartment?" I asked. "Yes. I came up to see if I could cut off the water for a few minutes." In the fluty voice she reserved for important matters, my mother had already tipped me off on his account: "I have a new worker, he's very nice, and he works well. He's Normand's son, you know, Normand Dupuis, who taught at the college with your father?" Powerless to erase the mark in the Egyptian carpet with the end of my shoe, I shrugged my shoulders. "Looks like it's going to stay there. I'm Karine." He shook my hand. "Louis. Nice to meet you." Just then my mother rushed into the living room, waving her CD of Charles Aznavour's greatest hits. "We have to play *La Bohème*! Put it in the pile. And I love your salmon mousse, what's the little taste?" I was flattered by the compliment. "It's horseradish, Mama." At the risk of coming across as old-fashioned, I was already happy that Louis should know I was a good cook. My mother was rearranging a few flowers in a vase on the piano. "Of course, Louis, you can cut the water for twenty minutes or so." Then she insisted he join the party, mentioning in passing that his father would be there as well. And so Louis came back at around seven o'clock with a bottle of Bordeaux and one of ice cider, dressed in black jeans and a white shirt with a Mao collar that made an impression even on the guests over sixty years old, all of whom were somehow inspired, that night, to have their kitchens renovated. In a corner of the dining room we talked about films, travel, and music groups. Just after midnight, he made an offer. "Can I take you home?" "Oh, that would be nice."

But how distant that was, I thought. I unscrewed the lid on the jar of strawberry jam, plunged my knife in a few times, and applied it to my croissant. I took a bite, with no appetite. Louis was now reading the first section of *La Presse*. How much time passed like this? I watched him, and crumbled bits of croissant onto the placemat. When I went to put the jam back in the refrigerator, I saw the 250-millilitre carton of milk on the counter, and a great weariness washed over me. I asked, "Why don't you buy milk in litres instead of these little boxes for Lilliputians?"

"Mmm?" he said, without raising his head. "Because I don't drink milk."

The croissant had left my hands greasy. I rinsed them over the sink under hot water, then I dried them on the dishtowel.

"No, no. It's just your way of doing things. You refuse to figure in my dentist's file, you don't want any trace of me in your fridge during the week. It's insulting!"

Louis' face screwed up as though I'd just thrust a rotten fruit under his nose. He got up, pushed away his chair, grabbed his empty cup, and passed in front of me. I said, "I'd like to know what your plans are, where we're going with this."

"It's my day off. Don't start."

He poured himself another coffee. I stayed next to the refrigerator. I looked at him, but he only stared at the caramel-coloured liquid flowing into his cup, and it was frustrating. We were strangers, each under an opaque glass bell.

"You have to tell me. Otherwise, I'm not sure I'm going to be interested anymore."

He studied me, perplexed. Then he turned off the espresso machine and sat back down with his cup, his eyebrows raised in disapproval. I thought to myself: "Karine, if he starts reading the paper again after what you've just said to him, you're out of here." So when Louis spread out the "Entertainment" section, I charged into his bedroom. I grabbed my slip and my bra off the unmade bed, I extricated my sweater and jeans from the big pile of dirty clothes on the floor. I asked myself: how can a thirty-six-year-old man who earns his daily bread vaunting the merits of foldaway food cupboards and full extension drawers complete

with separators ignore the invention of a wicker basket into which you can properly deposit your dirty
laundry at night? Then I understood: it was an im-
posture on his part – just one more.

I dressed quickly and I was just tying my hair up
in front of the mirror when Louis appeared in the
doorway:

"Karine?"

I tightened the elastic over my head.

"It's since that business of the dentist. We're not
in the same place. I think I want more than that."

He approached and sat on the edge of the bed.
The contour sheet was undone; he carefully pulled
the elastic over the corner of the mattress.

"I hate feeling trapped, that's all."

I stuffed my nightie and my makeup case into my
bag. Inside there were my clean clothes, those I would
have worn had the day unfolded calmly, which I realized was unlikely to happen.

"You felt trapped? Well you can be happy now, I'm
going."

"It's over?"

I couldn't answer that question. So as to leave him
the possibility of saving the situation, I invented an
imaginary object that was giving me trouble at the

bottom of my bag. But Louis was silent. Did he need a diagram? I said, "I can't stand uncertainty."

He nodded his head.

"I understand."

I thought, "That does it."

I approached him to get my lip balm from the bedside table. He clasped my forearm, then brought his hand down to mine.

"I'm sorry I disappointed you. Will you give me a kiss, at least, before leaving?"

I sucked on my lips very hard to keep from crying. I was also biting the insides of my cheeks. I didn't want to go anymore. Why hadn't we gone for breakfast to a restaurant that morning? A public place would have spared us this shipwreck. But I thought again. I still would have been tormented by the same questions. I started to panic. I squeezed his hand.

"Give you a kiss, for... Is it because you want me to stay?"

"It's your decision. But if you leave me, you can still kiss me one last time."

I fled into the entranceway. I pulled on my coat and I thrust my feet into my shoes without taking the time to do them up. How is it that Louis didn't run after me to stop me? I was the one who had to go back into the bedroom. He looked dejected, and hadn't moved a centimetre. I thought, all this happened without his even seeing it coming. I can at least give him a chance.

"But why, then, do you hope we'll still be together in a year?"

Without looking at me, Louis shook his head.

"I... Mmmf..."

I waited. He didn't move.

"Mmmf..."

I waited.

Then I went down the hall again and crossed the entranceway. The door slammed behind me and I felt the reverberation in my back and all the way into my heels.

"Call, call, call!"

All the rest of the weekend, like a piece of flotsam on my living-room couch, my telephone on my stomach, I repeated this prayer over and over. Sometimes I added "please," sometimes "bloody coward." The add-on depended on my condition, which was unstable. Was I the architect of my own unhappiness? The worst kind of relational twit? I didn't know. The telephone didn't ring. I had ulcers.

At the office, my pee breaks increased in number; at every opportunity I barricaded myself in the bathroom in the corridor behind the elevators to cry. My workmates thought I was suffering from a serious urinary infection. My boss bought me cranberry juice and refused to be reimbursed. In fact, I think people were just being discreet, because I had the eyes of a frog.

Outside, there was a warm spell that clashed visibly with my mood. When I spotted the first ant of the season climbing my kitchen wall, I called Louis so he would come and squash it. But I hung up before the first ring. At the hardware store, I bought ant traps, but a different brand from Raid.

Marlène came to visit. She brought Indian food that dribbled onto my placemats from their aluminum containers. She was proud of me, of my courageous act. Mischief in her eyes, she talked up Charles, Brian's good friend, a lawyer with a burgeoning career. She proposed a get together on her sun-washed terrace with a view across to Mount Royal. I was astounded:

"Charles? Haven't you already talked about him? The Jewish guy who eats bacon but insists absolutely on marrying a girl from his own faith?"

I sucked on a few grains of basmati rice while

Marlène reflected: "Yeah." She chewed a tandoori shrimp, asked me for a glass of water, and then confessed: that very Saturday afternoon, while they were looking for the perfect tennis racket, she and Brian had run into Louis at Sports Experts on Sainte Catherine Street. Marlène's tongue was clacking with indignation:

"I didn't want to tell you, but it might do you good. Two hours after you left him, the gentleman was still up for a shopping trip downtown!"

I thought that was still not as bad as Richard, who went off to sleep with a barmaid. But I don't want to make comparisons. My stomach was in knots. I said, "He's needed a new putter for a long time."

I joined my mother for a drink in a Park Avenue bar. She was scandalized at the idea of my breakup. She wouldn't be my age for anything in the world; what was the problem with men these days? Her students at university were the same; they wanted to have their cake and eat it too. "You can't spend all your life double parked," she asserted. "Sooner or later you have to get out of your car and put money in the meter!" I tried to decode this image – was I a parking meter? – but it was beyond me. She promised that we would go together to be fussed over at an Eastern Townships spa this summer, and in the meantime she insisted that her name be inscribed in my dentist's file. I replied:

"That's what's so ridiculous! Did you ever hear of someone having a heart attack while being flossed? Did you?"

But she insisted, and that's the way it always is with my mother:

"If they want an emergency number, there must be a reason!"

She grilled me on how much protein I was ingesting each day. I told her she was getting on my nerves. She didn't care. She paid for our drinks, and asked the waiter what the little taste was in the stuffed olives. It was cumin. On the way home, she was still expressing her astonishment that it wasn't fennel.

I don't know how many days went by. Fifteen? Twenty, perhaps. Now I was able to take down my garbage without keeping my cell phone on me so as not to miss his call – but since I had a read out and voicemail, I'm not sure that constituted real progress. Still, there was the afternoon at the office when I laughed myself silly along with my colleague Geneviève after Sébastien Charbonneau forwarded us the e-mails the marketing director had sent to the Romanian waitress at the Café Suprème. He'd vaunted the virtues of his Jacuzzi, waxed rhapsodic over her accent and the shape of her body, and urged her to go with him to a conference in the region of Charlevoix. There was a rumour that he'd been sacked, but another that the waitress had withdrawn her complaint. No matter. Geneviève and I were still laughing in the elevator, then in the subway. The smile had not left my lips when I turned the corner of my street, where green buds were transfiguring the trees. The rays of the setting sun warmed my face and throat. I thought, "What would you say to that, Louis Dupuis? I'm laughing to beat the band! I wonder what you'd say to that!" And it's then that I froze. On the sidewalk under my window, in front of his truck, his arms crossed over his chest, his dark glasses perched on top of his head, he was there.

"Hi Karine," he said, "Can we talk?"

MAN UNFAITHFUL,

WOMAN SAD

....

From: Bianca Larrivée
Subject: Olà!
Date: June 24
To: Maryse Gagnon

Olà, Maryse!

Here we are. The flight was perfect, the hotel is great, comfy and modern, it's sunny, 32 in the shade, I'm super relaxed. I know you have doubts and you'd never forgive Martin such a thing, but Philippe is sincere in what he's doing. As for me, even if it was a huge relief to get it all off my chest, I regret having spilt the beans because the last thing I'd want is for you to think badly of Philippe. Anyway, I just wanted to say that when you go by the apartment to feed Boris, don't let him out. He might take off and you'd be stuck there all night waiting for him to come back! Also, if you could water our basil plant (on the back balcony), it would be wonderful. Thanks a lot, dear friend. I won't write you again all week, we really want to be cut off from civilization.

Bianca x

P.S. Philippe wants Martin to know that he'll be free to play golf on July 15. If you like, we can spend the day together and do a barbecue with them in the evening.

P.P.S. I hope you can read this e-mail. The guy in charge of the "Business Center" here speaks a bit of English, and he told me they sometimes have encrypting problems.

From: Bianca Larrivée
Subject: Son of a...
Date: June 26
To: Maryse Gagnon

....

... bitch!! You were right, Maryse. I should have listened to you.

What an asshole! How could I have been so naïve as to think that his invitation to a four-star resort in Cancun would be enough for me to just forget the whole business? Yesterday I drank three or four mojitos too many (it's the only way to get the food down, it's all drowned in some orange glop that tastes of mouldy Tabasco). My feelings have come to the surface, and I've started asking myself questions again. WHY DID HE DO THAT? I feel like puking when I think of it, pictures exploding in my head. Philippe keeps claiming that he doesn't even know her last name and that he only saw her once, but really, in the twenty-first century, you don't screw someone without at least leaving them your cell number or e-mail after the fact, even just for appearance's sake. He swears on his mother's head that it isn't what I think, but she doesn't count, she's a crazy old loon. He says it was just sex. I'm so humiliated! In the end, I think I would have preferred not to know, because his whole lying argument comes down to that. He says, "Do you think I would have confessed if I'd had the slightest intention of doing it again?" The gentleman's patting himself on the back! He says I don't understand because we women, as soon as we sleep with a guy, our brain goes poof and we can't help starting to dream, he claims that our libido is a "fantasy machine." I've never heard anything so stupid! Whereas for men, it's natural to sleep with a woman "and then basta." I'd like to show him who's going to say basta to whom... Okay, the guy in the

Business Center is giving me signals, he's closing in five minutes for siesta, anyway there's never anyone here, just me, poor desperate me, come to lament my fate instead of taking advantage of the sun and the sea... But I've forgotten the best: Philippe told me that if I were not so possessive and controlling, he might not have given in to temptation and jumped the fence, because it all must have been "turning around in his head, at an unconscious level." Anything to avoid blame, to turn the situation against me! How am I going to bear this manipulator until Sunday? For the moment, he's gone to sulk on the beach with the latest novel by Frédéric Beigbeder, not surprising that he only thinks with his prick what with reading writers like that. I'm going to leave him. I have to leave him. Why is life always unfaithful men and sad women? Sad women and unfaithful men. An old stuck record since the beginning of time. Have you never thought about that? Okay, okay, I've resisted telling you for a long time because it's none of my business, but you know, last year, one night coming back from golf, Philippe told me that Martin had a colleague at his agency who "disturbed" him a lot... I don't know any more, maybe there's nothing to worry about, but if ever you broach the subject with him and things go badly, you have the key to my place, my friend, so feel free to make it yours. I'm going to kick Philippe out as soon as we get back on Sunday, and you and I could be housemates! Why not? Didn't you tell me that Martin had spent the night (really?) at his head accountant's after an office party last winter, on the pretext that he was too drunk to drive? Honestly, if I were you, I'd look into it. (Now that I think of it, there's a detail comes back: seems she looks like Nicole Kidman.) Damn, the supervisor is playing with his keys, I have to go! Just one more question: you know me, do you find me possessive and controlling? Be honest, after all, I'm on this earth so as to evolve. My God, I'm miserable. I'm going to try the Cardio-Latino course at the edge of the pool.

Bibi x

From: Bianca Larrivée
Subject: Don't worry
Date: June 28
To: Maryse Gagnon

My Dear Maryse,

I'm so sorry for the other day's psychodramatic e-mail. I'll have to start hoping that the system here really does have encrypting problems. Oof! The storm has passed. Philippe and I have decided to have children; at least two to start, but we wouldn't rule out three if things go well. I don't know if it's because of that, but since yesterday I've hardly even thought anymore about his misbehaviour. After all, one lapse in four years, it could be worse. You have to put things in perspective. And it's true that he's been honest with me, you can't take that away. I hope everything's okay between you and Martin. You know I don't think you should make anything out of what I wrote you last time. If my memory serves, she was just a young graduate from business school who had got a job in the Human Resources department, and he found her cute, that's all. And this business of Nicole Kidman, it's only because she dressed up as a Moulin Rouge can-can dancer for the annual costume ball, and that got everyone at the agency talking, right up to the CEO... So there's no big deal!

Thanks again for Boris and the basil.

Bianca x

P.S. For the barbecue on July 15, would it be all right if we invite Philippe's mother? She'll be passing through town that weekend with her new boyfriend, an engineer who's very nice.

From: Bianca Larrivée
Subject: What to do?
Date: June 30
To: Maryse Gagnon

I'm going crazy. I caught Philippe eyeing the behind of a customer waiting at the money-change counter, and the wound reopened. Meanwhile he wouldn't stop trying to make me believe that it only happened once, with the girl in the bar. He kept swearing on his mother's head until I screamed, change the record, anyway your mother is a broken-down basket case who digs up a different creep every three months on the Internet. Everything went downhill after that... I told him what I really thought, how do you expect me, Monsieur, to bring up children along with a liar, a hypocrite, someone as irresponsible as you? He went off alone on the high seas fishing boat excursion even though we'd reserved for two... Beside myself, I ran over here to write you. The supervisor asked me why I was crying, he said I was more beautiful when I was smiling... *smile, smile, Señorita...* it made me laugh... and one thing led to another... he locked the door to the Business Center and pulled down the shades... it happened so fast, you understand, I wasn't myself anymore. I ran to my room after it was over. Wow. Too bizarre. Now I'm all mixed up. Antonio... something like that... but Antonio who? No idea. Nothing. He didn't leave me his cell number or his e-mail address, so in the end I thought to myself, why would Philippe have done so with his poopsie (it's clear she was a poopsie)? Anyway, I'd love to see Antonio again before we leave here tomorrow morning, but for the first time all week he's not at his post, someone else has replaced him... I didn't know it, but he's also in charge of scuba diving here... I'm really on a cloud! Still, everything was starting to go a bit better with Philippe... But I have to leave you, I've got to go and take care of him, he's hunkered down in the room, he got seasick on the fishing boat, poor baby... At least he won't be up to much tonight, because compared to what I experienced this morning Ricky Martin moves like a Teletubby... How could I even describe it? I get one of those tremors in my gut every time I think of him. Ooh là là!... I'll call you as soon as we land, above all not a word of this to Martin, who knows what they talk about, our two little sweeties, between golf holes?

Bianca x

P.S. If you need a vacation, would you like it if we came back here, just you and me, next fall? I really exaggerated about the food.

ARE YOU MARRIED
TO A PSYCHOPATH?

When I said I was going to Rebecca's, Pierre didn't
understand why I wouldn't rather stay with Valérie.
My eldest daughter lived just a few streets away on
the South Shore, the house had a guest room, and I
could have helped her with the children in the
evening, given that Marc was working at night, what
with the hockey finals in full swing and the downtown in the throes of what looked like a revolution.
As for Rebecca, she lives in a little four and a half right
in the centre of the Plateau Mont-Royal, a lively urban
neighbourhood more than fifteen kilometres away.

There I would have to sleep on the folding bed in the living room, plus the fact that Rebecca worked odd hours, and my presence might be inconvenient if she came home late or had to get up really early.

"And then you can never find a parking space around there!" Pierre added.

That's why I cried "Bingo!" that morning as I backed up and twisted the wheels of my Jetta so as to squeeze in between a Jeep and a Plymouth with its FUCK BUSH bumper sticker, just under the winding staircase leading to the Mentana Street triplex where my daughter was renting the second floor. Because Pierre's apprehension had made me nervous. All the way in I kept asking myself: am I going to be turning in circles forever on the nearby streets, looking for a place to put my car? And if I can't find one, am I going to have to turn around, cross back over the bridge to the South Shore, while my whole plan goes up in smoke? By *plan* I of course mean spending some time with Rebecca, but above all organizing a reunion between her and Raphaël her childhood companion, the son of my great friend Murielle.

The cool morning air of April nipped at my cheeks. While I was getting my things out of the trunk, a tall man across the street, dressed in a striped suit, was trying to load his children into his Subaru. The arguments on which he drew – no more video games, the limits to his patience – weren't having much effect on the cries of his two little girls, their lunch boxes on the ground, their scarves tangled in the straps of their knapsacks. It occurred to me that I had not given Rebecca an exact time for my arrival, but it hadn't seemed to bother her: "You have to get here before ten o'clock so I can give you the extra set of keys," that was all she said. The Subaru was just disappearing at the end of the street when I arrived at the second-floor balcony whose wood facing was showing signs of rot. Rebecca came to the door. She had a green towel wrapped around her body, a red one wound about her head, and a cell phone glued to her ear; she gave me a kiss, one hand held over the phone.

"Oh, flowers!" she exclaimed.

She took me in her arms and told me it had been ages since anyone had brought her flowers, which immediately reassured me as to the correctness of my plan. Her body was warm and still thin and firm. I pulled the door shut behind me while she disappeared down the hall hopping on her toes, doubtless because of the chill air that had invaded the apartment. She continued her conversation in a singsong voice:

"Yes, my mother... oh... for a couple of days..."

In the living room, the first room after the tiny entranceway where my daughter's shoes and leather boots were all piled up, I put my suitcase on the floor and the bouquet of tulips on a low table next to a chipped coffee bowl, a jar of apple compote, and a pile of books, most of them open and face down to save the page. If my daughter was reading so much it's because she was a cultural journalist on a big Montreal daily, and every Saturday in "Section D" she turned into a literary critic, even though she kept insisting that no one was interested in what she said; at most, she claimed, they were happy just to count the stars at the bottom of the page. So I had to put her straight in no uncertain terms: "Well I, my dear, I read you faithfully, religiously!"

But that was nothing. What I most wanted to read was her novel, a gorgeous saga she'd talked about often before finishing her degree in literature. When she would finally produce it, I had no idea. Out of respect for that culture of secrecy that is supposed to be crucial to the creative act, I'd never broached the subject with her, which made me all the more eager to discover that world unfolding at the end of the seventeenth century, with its story of Mademoiselle

Anne, a *fille du roi* arrived in New France, who against all obstacles defies her fate and founds a school. I must say that I've always had a weakness for characters who are teachers; I was one myself before retiring the year before.

"Make yourself at home, Mom!" shouted Rebecca, from somewhere deep in the apartment. "I'm going to dress."

To get some light, I yanked open the beige cotton curtains with one quick tug, and it was just then that it happened. As usual, I wanted to fix my hair, and as there was no mirror in the living room, I had to go into the bathroom. There was the scent of soap and fruity shampoo in the air, while the fan was humming away wheezily. Since there was still enough humidity to turn my hair into a big ball of ringlets, I worked fast. But then: when I went to drop the few hairs caught in the teeth of my comb into the wastebasket near the basin, I froze. Perched on a pile of Kleenex there was a tube of sand-coloured latex, all soft, filled with a greyish liquid. I put my hand to my throat as the hairdryer began to purr in Rebecca's bedroom. I had never seen a condom close up like that, especially not a condom that had been put to use by my daughter, and I didn't know what irked me more: the fact that Rebecca had not told me she was seeing someone since her separation from Simon, or the fact that, not daring to deposit my hair on top of this condom that seemed – I would have sworn – still damp, I had to shove it into the inside pocket of my handbag. As if that wasn't bad enough, stretching my neck a little more, I saw the well-stuffed tip of another condom protruding from a tissue and hanging limply over the outside of the wastebasket.

I came out of the bathroom after a struggle with the doorknob, whose mechanism could have used a good oiling. Rebecca had changed into blue jeans and a white sweater with pagoda sleeves; her blonde hair fell over her delicate nape.

"I'm going to see Raphaël's photo exhibition this afternoon!" I announced, à propos of nothing. "It's a series on India this time."

Rebecca's only reaction was to take hold of the bouquet of tulips on the low table.

"Oh yes? Do you think I should cut the stems?"

I told her no, and she went to fill a vase with water, into which she plunged the flowers. She had to go to a press conference and would be back for supper. From the bathroom there came clickings that I guessed were generated by the cases for various cosmetics: face powder, eyeshadow, lipstick. I wondered whether my plan would still hold up after what I'd just discovered, and I decided in the affirmative; this relationship that she was keeping secret couldn't be serious. A passing fancy at the most. But oh my God, I thought to myself after a little more reflection; what if it was a man already involved with someone else? He had not, in any case, slept here, otherwise Rebecca would have told me to arrive any time after a certain hour, and not any time before ten o'clock.

"Pasta tonight, is that okay?" she cried.

An even more terrible idea went through my head: since there were two condoms, might that mean there were two men? That would be worse than anything. But no, I reasoned with myself, what a ridiculous hypothesis. I rummaged in my suitcase, looking for my slippers, while trying to sound chipper.

"I love pasta! Do you need me to do some shopping? I brought my own sheets, I knew you didn't have extra. I also brought your Pilates DVD, finally it didn't work for me. You know that your nephew and niece are taking yoga courses at the daycare? It's unbelievable!"

Her high heels hammered the wood floor as she came back into the living room to consult a paper filed in the Clairefontaine folder with blue squares perched on the corner of her desk, a walnut piece finished in the old style, that had belonged to her father. Her perfume tickled my nose, a mixture of mandarin and lavender. Rebecca gave me my key and told me there were croissants in the freezer and peppered ham in the refrigerator if I got hungry.

"Maybe later," I said.

"Okay, where the hell is my taxi?"

While I watched her shifting from foot to foot in front of the window, I could hardly keep myself from bursting out, "My darling, if that man is already taken, he's not a good choice!" It goes without question – yes, because that's the reason I'm there – that my daughter deserves a man who will care for her, repair her rotten balcony and oil her doorknobs, for example, to start with. So why does everything seem so complicated?

When Rebecca left Simon more than a year and a half ago, I had no doubt she'd made the right decision. As my daughter had lost ten pounds barely a few months after the beginning of her relationship with this popular actor twelve years her senior, I'd suspected for some time that she wasn't happy with him. And I saw the proof one August Sunday, the very day she turned thirty. So as to isolate himself while working on a film script, Simon had rented a chalet at Sainte Adèle for the summer, and because Rebecca was joining him on weekends, she suggested we celebrate her birthday there. It was a splendid morning, and we were all delighted at the idea of setting out for the Laurentians. Pierre and I in the Jetta, Valérie, Marc, and their children in the minivan. But once arrived we found Rebecca on the balcony facing the lake, sitting cross-legged on the chaise-longue. The site was wonderful: water was gurgling, the giant conifers were swaying in the breeze, and creamy clouds drifted across the sky. But my daughter was planted there, an old straw hat on her head, a water glass full of cigarette butts beside her, still dressed in an old T-shirt. We went up to her and finally surrounded her, feeling a bit out of place with our bags of food and our presents wrapped in brightly coloured paper. After casting an empty gaze on us, Rebecca started crying, staring out at the water. "Jesus Christ, what's wrong?" Marc finally blurted out – and for once, I must say that my policeman son-in-law's blunt words did not seem inappropriate to the situation. Rebecca wiped her tears on the oversized sleeve of her T-shirt, and sobbed, "We had a fight." And that's how my daughter celebrated her thirtieth birthday: her eyes swollen behind dark glasses, her complexion grey, unable to swallow even a mouthful of grilled sausage or macaroni salad. A real zombie, as Pierre said once we'd talked it all over a few days later. Only Morgane and Matisse were able to get a smile out of her when they offered her a giant card cut out of red cardboard and decorated with stickers of fairies and automobiles. When one of us ventured into the chalet to go to the bathroom or to look for some condiment in the kitchen, their return to the balcony was greeted each time by weighty stares whose implicit meaning was clear: "Did you see him? Is he there? Is he going to come out?" After lunch, Valérie asked Rebecca if she'd rather we left, but she rejected the idea. "No, stay, you're all I've got." And she at last told us what was going on. "Simon says I'm crazy." Around the table there was much frowning, clearing of the throat, sighs, and exclamations. "I've heard that you should never believe anyone who tells you you're crazy," Valérie said finally, while cleaning ketchup crust off the children's cheeks. My eldest daughter had studied psychology while at university, so we all went quiet to hear what would follow. Dipping the washcloth into a glass of water, she went on: "When someone accuses you of something, it's a projection. It's the old principle of 'What you say is what you are.' When you get down to it, it's in his head that something's not right." We all agreed with this theory. Of course, I thought, Simon must be the problem if he was treating my daughter this way on her birthday, and in front of her family, to boot. Why didn't the brute come out of his hiding place and put an end to this gloom that was making everyone so unhappy? It was only at the end of the afternoon, while I was helping Matisse catch butterflies along the rocky path bordering the chalet, that I heard Simon through a basement window, where Rebecca had told me he had set up his office so he could be cool. *Ha ha ha. It's the sheep who has been prophesying to me!*" I felt like going up to the window and shouting: "You boor! You ham! My daughter isn't crazy, and if Jean-Claude were here, you wouldn't be getting off so easily!" But then, what would my grandson Matisse have thought, who was already disappointed that his grandma was only trapping slobbery grasshoppers in her net, instead of beautiful butterflies? Not to mention Pierre, who would certainly not have appreciated my reminding him of how Jean-Claude, with his legendary daring, would have dealt differently with the situation. The only initiative Pierre had taken all day was to light the barbecue. But of what importance all that? The following month Rebecca left Outremont and Simon's house and took back her apartment on Mentana that she'd sublet for a year to a young Parisian girl studying the cello at McGill University. So I said to myself, my daughter's bound to find someone else. If I did, after Jean-Claude's car accident, why not her?

That's what I thought.

There was a honking out on the street, and Rebecca gave me a kiss on the cheek.

"My taxi is here!"

"See you tonight, dear."

The door slammed. I went into the kitchen, found the garbage can under the sink, and tossed in the clump of hair I'd been keeping in my handbag.

In the middle of the wide space with its caramel wood floor, behind a glass counter where African-style jewellery was on show, a young girl in her early twenties was on guard.

"Do you know the artist?"

She had an English accent and she eyed me coldly. For a moment I regretted coming on foot to this Old Montreal gallery, and, for comfort's sake, having worn my exercise clothes and sneakers. I must have looked like a tourist. But for some time I'd been enjoying long walks. Every Sunday I took off along the paths of Mont Saint-Hilaire along with a dozen enthusiasts like myself. Some in the group were so addicted that they were training for a pilgrimage to Santiago de Compostela, while insisting there was nothing remotely spiritual in their initiative. This seemed strange to me; if that's the case, I thought, why not just go on an excursion at Mont Tremblant or in the Adirondacks? But it was none of my business, and while the imperious young woman continued to stare me down, I determined not to be intimidated. So I glared right back at the silvered satin tunic she was wearing over a pair of black leggings, as though it was the most ridiculous outfit I'd ever seen.

"I'm a friend of the family," I replied.

Immediately, her face relaxed.

"Oh yes? He shouldn't be long. What he does is very beautiful. Would you like some green tea?"

I accepted her offer, and after vanishing for a few seconds into what looked like a storage room at the back of the gallery, the young woman returned with a porcelain cup resting on a saucer. I continued my tour of the premises while blowing on the hot liquid.

Out of devotion to the memory of my great friend Murielle, who had been carried off by an aggressive cancer three years earlier, I made it my duty to attend all the photo exhibitions of her only son, to which I was invited by e-mail along with a hundred or so others. *Au bout du monde/End of the World* was Raphaël's third show in two and a half years, and the way people lived in India seemed even more astonishing than what went on in Bolivia or Thailand, the two countries he'd previously trekked through with his camera. In India, skeletal bearded men strode totally naked through the streets (*Sâdhu*, photo 4), women did their laundry in a brown-watered Ganges (*Twilight*, photo 18), and children no older than my grandchildren put together jasmine garlands for the tourists (*Daily Bread*, photo 22). Raphaël had captured all that on film, and what is more, judging by the little red dots on some of the descriptive labels to the right of the photos, his work was being very well received.

I occasionally got news of Raphaël through his father, Antoine, when Pierre and I invited him to supper, which, I must admit, happened less frequently since he'd taken up with Maria, a Spanish-speaking real estate agent with false nails. "If Murielle could see that!" I exclaimed the first time he came over with her. "Who are you to judge?" Pierre had said, in such peremptory fashion that I was sure he was thinking that Antoine, too, must have compared him with Jean-Claude the first time he saw me by his side. In any case, the last we heard of Raphaël was a month earlier, when Antoine informed us that his son had broken up with Marjorie, his long-time girlfriend. It was that night, while Maria was raving about the spa she'd had installed in her Tuscan-style garden in Repentigny, that I began to think about my plan.

Of course, Murielle and I had talked about that possibility hundreds of times: wouldn't it be wonderful if Raphaël and Rebecca were to form a couple one of these days? As there were only a few months between them, for the two young mothers we were it seemed like a natural idea. We wheeled them side by side in their carriages, we put them to bed for their naps at the same time, and often, when we went to wake them, we found their two warm little bodies huddled one against the other. And what about all the summer vacations at Cape May or Cape Cod when Murielle persuaded Antoine to abandon his patients for a few days and I succeeded in doing the same thing with Jean-Claude and his litigations? On the beaches crawling with vacationers, all it took was for a child to threaten to throw water in Rebecca's face, or to kick down her sand castle, for Raphaël to launch into an imitation of his favourite superhero, The Hulk, and to ward off the little troublemaker. Of course, they'd drifted apart during adolescence, and there'd been a lot of water under the bridge, but there you are: since they're both now thirty years old and alone with no children, isn't that proof that they'd never been able to come up with anyone better than the little soulmate they'd been for one another?

"Isn't that a good idea, Muriel?" Because it's our long conversations I've missed most since she left, I often find myself talking to my good friend in my thoughts. Of course, I sometimes go for a coffee with Linda Guénette, my former colleague, or for a glass of wine with Brigitte Lemaître, a promiscuous divorcée from my walking club, but it's not the same.

The young girl put a CD into the stereo on the shelf behind her, and the speakers spat out a few guitar notes. I went to give her back my teacup, and she again disappeared behind the door at the back of the gallery. She had still not returned when Raphaël made his appearance dressed in jeans ripped at the knees, a black shirt open on a red T-shirt, dark glasses with silver frames on his nose, his face as smooth as ever. I went right up to him.

"Raphaël, my sweet, bravo! You take me around the world!"

He took off his dark glasses:

"Hey, Lucie! Great to see you, you look fantastic!"

That's what I liked about Raphaël: he always compensated for his brooding adolescent exterior with a well-chosen compliment. I kissed his cheeks:

"So, they're selling like hotcakes?"

"Bah, nothing but tourists looking for souvenirs. But I'm not complaining. Sharon is out back?"

"The little salesgirl? Yes, I think so."

He asked me to wait, and went off towards the back of the gallery.

"Did you get my e-mail?" I cooed, before he had quite disappeared. "Are you free for a coffee?"

He left the door partly open behind him. From time to time bits of conversation reached me, but because of the guitar I couldn't make them out clearly. A man in his seventies with a fanny pack around his waist pushed open the door of the gallery, stared blankly inside, then regained the sidewalk and continued on his way in the company of a stocky woman sucking at an ice cream cone, despite the chilly weather.

In the tea room on Saint Paul where Raphaël suggested we go, there were a number of impressive plants on the windowsills that would have been right at home in a greenhouse. As he hadn't had lunch, he ordered, along with his café au lait, a roast pork and marinated eggplant panini. I took a cranberry biscuit.

Raphaël said that what he had brought back from his trip to India was a deep feeling that the present moment was the sole barometer of human happiness.

"Isn't that what I do with my photos, capture the moment?" he remarked.

I found this observation a little naïve, but I let him go on. He said that what he'd also developed down there was a pronounced affinity for slowness, and as he lingered over the description of a Hindu temple some three hours out of Calcutta, whose photograph he had submitted to a contest sponsored by an important French magazine, I found myself growing impatient.

"I don't want to jump from one thing to another, my dear, but are you busy tomorrow night?"

"I don't think so."

"Would you like to have dinner with Rebecca and me? We're having our kitchen renovated in Brossard, so I'm spending a few days with her."

Raphaël frowned.

"Rebecca, your daughter?"

I tried not to squirm too much in my seat.

"Who else?"

He took a thoughtful bite out of his panini, and then, after chewing it calmly, said:

"It must be ten years since I've seen her."

I didn't want to revive painful memories, but I corrected him, reminding him that they had crossed paths at Murielle's funeral.

"That's possible," Raphaël sighed. "I was really out of it that day! I'd taken too many tranquillizers."

"Me too."

"But it's coming back. She was there with Simon Ouellette, the actor?"

"Oh, that's all in the past. It's all over! Simon was never interested in anything but his navel."

Raphaël grimaced.

"That's what my ex said about me."

I brushed the crumbs from my biscuit off the table.

"You know, Raphaël... you know that Rebecca is a cultural journalist? Have you seen her articles in the paper?"

Raphaël was grinding away at the slice of eggplant between his teeth.

"I never read the newspapers. They're all lies, just tools to manipulate the people."

The oil had made his lips shine purplish pink. He dabbed at them with his napkin and I decided we'd talked enough about Rebecca for the moment. So I was asking him if I might buy a copy of his photo number 3, the one showing a little monkey dipping his hand into a big bag of chips, when his cell rang. After grunting into the phone and scratching the back of his neck with his silver-ringed thumb, Raphaël hung up and said he had to go back to the gallery to meet a couple of Americans who were interested in his pictures.

"What did I tell you," he added. "Nothing but tourists."

"Your mother would be so proud of you!"

Raphaël left, swallowed up by the clinging ivy over the door.

Later that evening, while we were finishing up our spaghetti putanesca in her cramped kitchen with the broken exhaust, it was Rebecca's turn to frown:

"We're eating with Raphaël tomorrow? What's the occasion?"

"What? I just thought it would be nice to get together. He's been on his own for a while."

I tried to discern a glimmer of interest on Rebecca's face. She was gnawing on a black olive.

"Wouldn't he rather watch the hockey game? It's the finals."

She spit the pit into her hand before depositing it on the edge of her plate.

"Raphaël is an artist, you know. He never even brought it up. I arranged for us to meet at a restaurant after the cocktails. I thought you would be pleased to see him again."

She screwed up her face.

"I would have preferred it to be just the two of us tomorrow night."

I was touched. I placed my hand over hers to caress it:

"But my dear, it's just the two of us tonight, no?"

When I'd got back from Old Montreal, I'd noticed that my daughter had emptied the wastebasket in the bathroom. Did she suspect that I must have seen what was inside? Would it ever be appropriate to bring it up with her? Her cell phone on the table started to vibrate, which startled me to the point where I jerked my wineglass and got a few drops onto the sleeve of my blouse. Rebecca unfolded her phone and a smile appeared on her lips as she took in what was on the screen.

"Something funny?" I asked, as I retrieved the salt shaker from over the stove.

"It's a text."

Her voice was distant. A while ago, I'd seen a report on this flourishing mode of communication that was making young people's spelling more hapless than ever, and I thanked God that I was now retired. I sprinkled salt onto my sleeve while eyeing my daughter, mesmerized by the screen on the phone poised over her plate of pasta.

Despite Rebecca's offer to let me use her bedroom for the rest of my visit, I chose to stay in the living room. I wasn't unhappy sleeping on a sofa bed with squeaky springs, this makeshift installation made me feel like I was on vacation, on a camping trip. A little after midnight, loud voices mixed with cries roused me from my light sleep. Dragging myself out from between the sheets, tying my bathrobe around my waist, slipping my feet into my slippers, I peered through the curtains. The street was dark, but on the steps of the triplex across the street three young men were smoking cigarettes and drinking cans of beer. It was a rather diverting spectacle. When, unable to sleep, I sometimes got up in the night at our house in Brossard to make myself some herbal tea in the kitchen, the silence always reinforced my sense of isolation, and there was nothing to see in our yard but the bird feeder.

Rebecca appeared at my side. She was wearing a red bandanna with white polka dots in her hair, and the low-hung yoga pants I'd given her at Christmas.

"Your neighbours seem rather tipsy," I remarked. "Did they wake you too?"

"Not really, I was reading," she sighed, as we observed the three overexcited young men on their front steps. "It must be the end of the semester. Or hockey fever. You see that one, the blond, with his coat open and the panties around his neck? He's a medical resident in gynecology."

In the darkness, it was difficult to make out details. I narrowed my eyes until the young man in question staggered into the pool of light the street lamp was casting over the stairs.

"My heavens, you're right... It's underwear!"

"They should have gone to a strip club."

I shook my head while the young man butted his cigarette in the metal pail next to the door.

"Do you still keep your appointment each year with Doctor Brissette?"

"Mama!"

"What? It's very important."

The trio of merrymakers went inside, and we went back to our beds.

Before losing hers, Murielle said that after the age of fifty women should pay a lot of attention to their hair, because of all the parts of the body it was without doubt the one that best resisted the passage of time, as long as one took care of it, and was careful with its colour.

So the next day, as the sun was going down, while I was applying finishing touches to my appearance, I thought of her while admiring my own hair. I asked her, "How do you find it?" It seemed perfect: both straight and full, shiny, the ends curled round to enclose my cheeks, the bangs swept into a well-defined wave on the side. "I'd like to look like Jackie Kennedy when she was First Lady, you know what I mean?" Those were my instructions that afternoon to the hairdresser with hairy hands at the Saint Lawrence Boulevard salon where Rebecca had made me an appointment. The music was loud and the hairdresser had frowned, curling his thick lips. "Jackie Kennedy! Jackie Kennedy!" he cried, very concerned. And yet the result was even more wonderful than I could have hoped. I was delighted. It's not every day that I'm invited to the launching of a magazine, nor that I reunite my daughter with her childhood friend in hopes of producing a few sparks, or, who knows, a fireworks display.

I was making up my eyelids in the bathroom when the doorbell rang. I went to see who it was. The man on the balcony was inspecting the rotten wood with a placid air. It took me a few moments to recognize him; it was the tall brown-haired man in the striped suit, the same I'd seen the previous day herding his children into his car, the only difference being that now he was wearing blue jeans and a leather coat.

"Yes?" I said.

Up close, he seemed older. You could make out a network of wrinkles in the folds at the corners of his eyes, and the ghost of a beard that dusted his cheeks with grey. He held out his hand:

"Mrs. Leclerc? I'm Vincent, a friend of Rebecca. I live just underneath."

I felt a chill current of air climbing up my nylon stockings under my sheath dress.

"Oh," I chirped, shaking his hand. "Nice to meet you."

"And you. I saw you arriving yesterday morning.

Rebecca told me you'd be spending a few days with her. That's your car parked in front?"

I had to stretch my neck to see the street over the balcony railing. Vincent was pointing to my Jetta. As I'd gone everywhere by foot since my arrival, it was still where I'd left it the day before.

"That's mine. Why?"

He rubbed the end of his nose on the worn sleeve of his leather coat before informing me that as of April 1, the city cleaned the west side of the street between five-thirty and six-thirty on Tuesday night, and I had to move my car if I didn't want to get a ticket. As a matter of fact, while Vincent was talking, I saw that only my Jetta was left on this side, and, a little farther down, a Toyota. I glanced at my watch, which showed five-twenty-five, and I stifled a "damn!" I'd planned to leave Rebecca's apartment at five-thirty and to make my way downtown in a taxi, to avoid the commotion prior to the playoff hockey game which, according to the news report at noon, was going to clog the streets.

"That's really bad timing!" I said, very put out by this unforeseen problem, and half-forgetting Vincent was there.

"In any case," he went on, "I thought you should know. Rebecca has no car, so she probably doesn't know about the regulation."

Five minutes later, having pulled on my sneakers over my nylon stockings, (you do what you have to, I'd decided) I climbed into my Jetta to cruise the nearby streets. On most of them the same restriction was in effect, so that the cars were lined up bumper to bumper on the side where it was legal to park. The only free places were reserved for those with parking stickers. When I finally saw a spot under a silver maple, I floored the accelerator, only to find, once I was at the right level, a fire hydrant on the sidewalk. "Damn and damn!" The streets were all one way, and they only had one lane. The cars were moving slowly, stopping at each corner to let pedestrians go by, most of whom, judging by their clothes and their laptop bags, were on the way home from work. Need I mention that Pierre chose just that moment to call me on my cell phone?

"Where are you?"

"In my car. I have to move it. They're cleaning the street. It's horrible, I've been turning in circles for fifteen minutes! And don't tell me what you're going to tell me."

"I told you so."

"I'm hanging up."

"Where's the cheque for the plumber?"

I lost track of the number of streets I'd tried. Time

was passing on my Jetta's clock face, and as if the quest for the urban Grail wasn't enough to make me late, at the corner of Boyer and Mount Royal I found myself boxed in by a traffic jam caused by the spectacle of a hunchbacked tramp being arrested by two policemen at the exit of the supermarket. The man was dressed in rags; his skin was grey, and even from some metres away his eyes were so glazed that you would have thought they were two holes blocked up by mirrors. Normally, when I see policemen at work, I think of my son-in-law Marc; were they from the same station? Did they know each other? Is it from them that he gets his store of unbearable vulgar jokes? But now I wasn't thinking about that. Looking at the tramp, who was so dirty that the policemen had to put on gloves just to approach him, I couldn't help thinking, "Why is this smelly beggar, this lurching human wreck, why is he alive? Why didn't he die in a car accident or eaten away by cancer? What would it have mattered?" While the policemen were ordering him to open his backpack, it became more and more clear to me that fate would do well to revise its selection criteria. "Who would it have bothered if it had been him that died?" I kept repeating. I knew my attitude was unforgivable, that it was utterly lacking in compassion and contrary to the principle of loving one's neighbour that I'd tried to teach my students for more than thirty years. Perhaps to stifle all that, I leaned on my horn, with some of the other drivers following my example, although an unhappy pedestrian, a boy of twenty, brushed against the hood of my car and twiddled his index figure over his temple, spitting out words that I couldn't understand.

A few minutes later I was back at my starting point. Tough luck, I'd decided; so I'll get a fine. It was almost six o'clock. The Toyota was gone, so that my Jetta would now be the only car in violation of the municipal regulations. Just as I was rushing up the winding staircase, Vincent came outside. His eyes went wide with incredulity when he saw my car in the same place.

"What do you want, it's blocked in everywhere!" I yelled down between the wrought-iron bars of the handrail.

I had to go back in to my daughter's to put on my heels and call a taxi. I'd just closed the door behind me when someone rang. It was Vincent again; he was turning his keys around in his pudgy fingers.

"Listen, Mrs. Leclerc, here's what we'll do," he declared. "I'm going to the hockey game and I'm parked on the right side of the street. You just have to take my place."

I almost burst out, "For goodness' sake, you could have thought of that earlier!"

"But you won't find anything downtown, they said so on the news!"

Vincent said that he worked in an office tower on René Lévesque Boulevard, and he had a place reserved for his car, day and night.

"In that case, I'll be right down. Let me just call a taxi."

He scratched his temple with the end of a key:

"By the way, where are you going?"

"To the Ritz, on Sherbrooke."

A few moments later he was climbing into his car and me into mine, and after a bit of manoeuvring I was on the good side of the street, and we were both in his Subaru, driving along Rachel Street. I explained to Vincent that I was going to the launching of a new magazine on which my daughter was collaborating. "Really, thank you," I kept muttering, while he went through orange lights, giving me little tingles of excitement, and even some regret at not having lived a more adventurous life these last years. It's true that had it been up to me, I would have preferred going on a trip to renovating the kitchen. "Why don't we go to Morocco?" I'd suggested to Pierre. "I saw a report the other day on TV. It's exotic." But Pierre had other ideas. We even argued about it, so that to annoy him a little, I'd threatened to join up with the other members of my walking club, and go off on my own on a pilgrimage to Santiago de Compostela. "Fine!" Pierre said, mockingly. "That will be good for your soul." And he went to fill his bird feeder with a mix of seeds.

Vincent talked easily, and perhaps because there were crushed Mini-Wheats and Clementine peels with their rancid fragrance all over his car floor, he spoke mostly about his life as a single parent. So that before we'd even got as far as Pine Avenue, I knew that his two little girls were adjusting well to shared parenthood, and that he still had a good relationship with his former partner, who worked in the restaurant business.

Once we were under the Ritz's awning, Vincent refused the twenty-dollar bill I offered him.

"But take it!" I protested, shaking it strenuously. "Without you, I'd have a fine plus a taxi fare to pay!"

Vincent recoiled even more. He squeezed his back against the door and lifted his forearms, agitating them in front of his chest like a little bird in distress. "No question!" he protested. I thought it was unfortunate that our trip should end like that, but it seemed just too ungrateful not to give Vincent something for his help. So I threw the bill onto the dashboard:

"Buy a little something for your daughters!"

Pandora: that was the name of the magazine whose cover for the first issue (the rather unusual photo of a well-rounded redhead with wide emerald eyes) was displayed on an easel just as you came through the hotel's revolving doors.

About fifteen years earlier, I'd visited the Ritz with Jean-Claude on the occasion of the bar mitzvah of the son of Mister Robert Levine, who was in the same law office as my husband. I had mixed memories of the event, where we felt a little bit like outsiders, perhaps because most of the guests were Anglophones, and we couldn't be sure of grasping all the subtleties in the speeches of the celebrants who went to the microphone and made everyone roar with laughter. Still, we had a fascinating discussion about the Holocaust with a Francophile couple at our table, the Blooms from Chicago, if I remember correctly. The woman, around fifty, with thick features, wore a baroque two-stringed pearl necklace, and her husband, apparently an accomplished tennis player, was a professor of history at the university. I'd had the impression that this exchange had somewhat compensated for the feeling of isolation we'd experienced during the rest of the evening, but on the way home, Jean-Claude had expressed a very different point of view. He claimed that old Bloom was just coming on to me. I had to be blind not to see it, and I should know better than to behave like an ignorant student who swallows the words of the first professor to come along. I told Jean-Claude to be quiet, but he even added: "In any case, Lulu, do you think you'd like that, to have it off with a Jew? A bald prick. Ha ha ha!" I hated it when his ideas became so crude. "J-C, you're drunk as a skunk!" I protested. "Keep your eyes on the road!"

I must say that my husband's behaviour around that time was becoming more and more unpredictable, without my knowing why. Whether it was the weather, the way his steak was cooked in a restaurant, or an electrician being late, anything at all could set him off and plunge him into a black mood. I went through all the classic questionings of a wife in that situation. Was he unhappy at work? Had he lost money? Did I still satisfy him? Was there another woman in the picture? What was behind that receipt from the Sheraton Hotel for more than three hundred dollars that I found in the inside pocket of his jacket? I'd shown it to Murielle, who cautioned me not to talk to him about it. "Let it go," she advised me. In her opinion, if it was something the least bit important, it would come out soon enough. So the months went by without anything happening, but without Jean-Claude's moods becoming any the less erratic, which came to worry me more than the idea that he might have had an extramarital adventure – a hypothesis that I never, one way or the other, sorted out.

In any case, even if Murielle and I often said to each other that it would be pleasant to come here for a cup of tea in the afternoon, I'd never set foot in the Ritz since the Levine boy's bar mitzvah. The ceiling lights in the lobby were dimmed just enough to give off a yellowish and velvety illumination, and the marble floor was so polished that it looked oiled. On every wall there were huge mirrors, creating the illusion that the bouquets of flowers rising out of the bulbous vases on the consoles, the chests of drawers, the writing desks, and the antique tables, seemed even more luxuriant than they were. I followed the direction in which the arrow on the easel was pointing. At the door to the room where the launch was taking place, there was a swarm of cameramen and journalists milling about with their assortment of microphones, booms, wires, and lights.

"Do you have your invitation?" inquired a woman in a dress whose low-cut neckline was edged with green lace.

I plunged a hand into my bag and the girl exchanged my card for a copy of the magazine. I rolled it up and tucked it under my arm. I did the same thing with my coat, and pushed my way through the crowd in search of Rebecca. Most of the guests were murmuring to each other, their faces hidden behind their glasses of wine, paying scant attention to the skinny creature, who, onstage, in front of windows draped with taupe velvet curtains, was talking into a microphone. In a quavery voice, she explained that *Pandora* was "the new magazine for today's new woman," and now we just had to hope that people would take up the challenge of this new femininity that wasn't afraid to tell things the way they were. After having expressed her pride at being the first editor in chief of *Pandora*, she thanked the sponsors, those generous partners who were supporting them in their initiative to provoke debate and to question society. In the litany that followed, I recognized a brand of dishwashing soap, one of shampoo – that I had already tried, and disliked – one of toilet paper, and another of vitamin juice, after which I lost track because I finally spotted Rebecca, and rushed up to her.

Dressed in leather boots that hugged her calves, a brown skirt, and a beige top with the sleeves rolled up, her hair twisted into a bun, my daughter was standing beside a fifty-year-old man with a face like a bat, and a mulatto of about thirty who, her nose plunged into her glass of wine, was casting a circular gaze over the assembled company. During the applause that followed the speech, Rebecca complimented me on my hair, and asked me how my appointment had gone with her hairdresser on Saint Lawrence Boulevard. I had just picked the last glass of wine off the tray of a passing server, when the editor in chief of *Pandora* appeared at our side.

"How was I? I really need a cigarette!"

"Perfect!" Rebecca assured her. "I'd like to introduce my mother, Lucie. Lyne, Mama."

I shook the woman's cold and bony hand.

"Congratulations on the magazine," I trilled, for lack of anything else to say.

Her blue eyes, encrusted in a thick layer of mascara, sparkled with a thousand lights.

"Your daughter has given us a sublime text. You should never have any regrets about your former son-in-law!"

I wasn't sure I'd heard her right.

"I beg your pardon?" I said.

Rebecca exchanged a conspiratorial smile with Lyne, whose whole body was bobbing back and forth. She grabbed Rebecca by the arm, and said again that she'd die if she didn't get a cigarette right then and there.

"Is it okay if I go with her, Mama? Do you have a glass? I'll be right back."

Some musical chords were being struck up inside the room. I was a bit confused.

"No, no, but... we're having dinner with Raphaël afterwards, you haven't forgotten?"

Rebecca and Lyne walked briskly towards the exit; a man of about twenty accosted them, but without breaking her stride, Lyne signed to him that she'd be back in five minutes, spreading wide her gnarled fingers and wiggling them over his head.

Finding myself alone in the crowd, I suddenly felt dizzy. As I didn't know anyone, I felt like I was paddling in a swimming pool without touching bottom, and there was no ladder, nowhere to catch my breath.

My coat and my copy of *Pandora* under my arm, my glass of wine in my other hand, I wended my way back through the assembled company and left the room. In the hallway leading to the lobby, the journalists and cameramen were packing up their equipment. I spotted a squat armchair away from the action, and sat myself down.

This wasn't the first time Rebecca had collaborated on a magazine. From time to time she had published interviews of important cultural figures from here and abroad. Usually she wasn't too happy with the results. "They change my texts so they look like they were written by a machine, and they cut the most important parts!" But it paid. However, turning the pages of *Pandora*, I wasn't sure what to expect. Why had this Lyne made allusion to Simon? Had Rebecca interviewed him? This idea, which seemed bizarre, didn't stay with me for long, because I soon came to page 27.

In an introductory text, it was explained that "Are You Married to a Psychopath?" was a forum offered to women who wanted to share with others "what they had to endure through love for a man." The idea was born from the realization that there were many women who, as soon as they got together, spent most of their time "finding fault with men: with their behaviour, their obsessions, their moods, their opinions, their hygiene." And so it was high time that a forum be made available to all those who wanted to take up their pen and shed light on the failings of the man with whom they'd lived – or, why not, with whom they were still living. At the end of the year, the readers would be invited to vote on the magazine's Internet site, and choose their favourite account, in other words the one that offered them the greatest consolation for their own "disenchantment," because the sad truth is, and it cannot be said too often, that Prince Charming does not exist. "So, since we're getting it in the neck," the introduction concluded, "why not get it off our chests a little as well!"

"How simplistic," I thought.

"Madame, a little wine?"

A server with bottles was negotiating the corridor between the lobby and the ballroom. I allowed him to fill my glass, and I took a big gulp.

A Portrait of *Homo vedettus*
By Rebecca Leclerc

For three years, I shared the life of a humorist-actor-host-screenwriter, and who knows what else? No doubt about it, my man was a star. Does that make you dream, ladies? The problem is that in this day and age, even going out with a *Homo anonymus* is very complicated. Now, these complications are magnified when the object of your affection is a *Homo vedettus*. So let us, together, demythologize this fascinating creature, because, as Hegel put it so well, "No man is a hero to his valet" — or, if you wish, "No man is a star for the woman who sleeps with him."

The night you first lay eyes on *Homo vedettus*, you find him even cuter than on the glossy paper of the gossip magazines you riffle through while standing in line at the grocery store. However, you can't go up to him, nor smile at him, nor spill your vodka and cranberry juice over him, because *Homo vedettus* might then confuse you with a *Star suckerus*, one of those vulgar female parasites that circulate in groups, and that feed on semen — an exercise to which many of his ilk will lend themselves when there's no better alternative. By chance, your *Homo vedettus* is not long in expressing his own interest. Is it possible that, accustomed to being desired and adored by all, *Homo vedettus* is immune from that legendary fear of rejection afflicting *Homo anonymus*? Braving the crowd, brushing aside your friends, he comes right up to you.

"You're beautiful, what's your name?"

Your first encounters unfold according to the rules of the game. A few films, a few intimate dinners. In the restaurants, when you get there first, you have to spar verbally with the waitresses to obtain a drink of water. But no sooner does *Homo vedettus* sit down opposite you than they start inquiring about the temperature of your soup and the texture of your tartare, leaving you deeply disillusioned with the feminine psyche. *Homo vedettus* talks to you about his childhood, his travels, his projects. As soon as you open your mouth, he interrupts you with a dreamy air:

"You're so beautiful!"

You find that charming. Wherever you go, aperitifs and digestifs are on the house. Are you losing your critical faculties? You are twenty-seven years old.

Soon, you reveal your new flame's name to your friends. Here, admit it: the little show-off in you is already basking in their reactions. However, once the surprise wears off ("Whoooooo? Oh wow, whooooooo, him?"), your friends start pulling faces. Everyone has a story to tell: the astronomical number of women he's bedded, what shameful diseases he's let himself in for. You deny everything. Nasty rumours. Still, seeds of doubt are sown.

"Dear, is it true that two years ago you hung out at B****
and that each night you brought a different girl home?"

"I'm a public figure. There are all sorts of rumours circulating about me. That I'm gay, for example. You'll have to get used to it."

"You're right."

"Don't listen to spiteful gossip."

"I promise. By the way, when was your last doctor's appointment?"

He gives you DVDs of films and television series in which he's played a role, he has you read texts he's written. When he's interviewed on TV or the radio he comes back rigid with anxiety, sure of having said too much about this or too little about that. You reassure him.

"You were perfect. The host didn't ask the right questions."

A gala is in the offing. A huge television extravaganza. Should you buy a dress? Not so fast. *Homo vedettus* insists that he never mixes his private life with his professional pursuits. In any case, he doesn't want to be seen by your side at a media event. He pours scorn on those in his circle who, every year, parade under the lights with their better halves. He urges you to understand: it's to protect himself, but above all to protect you, his most precious object of affection, his treasure, his little lamb who is too pure to deal with the shallow celebrity jungle. And so you watch the gala on television dressed in your polka dot pyjamas. The next day, *Homo vedettus* begs you not to be alarmed if you come across a photo in the newspapers showing him side by side with a vivacious young girl; he's been snapped on the red carpet along with his agent's new assistant. His gift for inconsistencies fascinates you. Contrite, *Homo vedettus* sweeps you off to a lovely inn in the Eastern Townships, where the sociologist in you observes that that there really are two solitudes in *la Belle Province*, because *Homo vedettus* is totally unknown to the Anglophone staff and clientele.

He is obsessed with his work. Often, at night, he gets up to jot down ideas. During the day he develops them, refines them, declaims them, faxes them to his agent. What goes on behind the closed door of his office? Sometimes he emerges euphoric, sometimes melancholy, sometimes amnesiac.

"It's your sister's birthday tonight? Ah no, my angel, I couldn't have told you I was going. I need my peace and quiet. And besides, I'm not going out with your family, but with you."

An ocular problem requires you to make an appointment with an ophthalmologist, who asks you to come accompanied, because to make a diagnosis he has to inject your eye with a liquid that will blur your vision. *Homo vedettus* agrees to go with you. Then, that morning, he changes his mind.

"I have to sleep some more. I need to be alert this afternoon. I'm giving two interviews."

"But I need you! I'm going to be half-blind in the middle of town when I get out of there!"

"I'm in the midst of a promotional campaign! You know

what that's like, dearest, the stress of a promotional campaign? Can you try to understand? Call your mother!"

It is eight-thirty. Your appointment is for ten o'clock. You call a girlfriend. In the waiting room, there is a pile of newspapers. You come upon a profile of your *Homo vedettus*, who speaks in rhapsodic terms about love and the couple.

"Did you see that?" you whimper. "What would you do in my place?"

"He's a narcissist," your girlfriend says. "Leave him."

You move in with him. Even though many *Homo vedettus* take pride in showing off their culinary skills on Josée de Stasio's cooking show or *Ricardo et compagnie*, you've drawn the short straw. Your *Homo vedettus* doesn't know how to cook an egg — literally. Is that the fault of the film-set caterers that have been feeding him all these years, prolonging his infantile status? At night, you concoct little dishes for him while he indulges in his favourite activity: watching television. Most of the time *Homo vedettus* looks at television to study his peers — or, like all Cro-Magnons, to watch hockey. But at that hour, his concern is to analyze the quiz shows dealing with popular culture: *Homo vedettus* wants to know whether his most recent creation — or why not, the entire body of his work — has made him prominent enough for his name to figure in the answer to a question that might enrich some ordinary man or woman to the tune of three hundred beautiful dollars. One night, it happens. He whoops for joy in the living room. You sigh over your cooking pots.

"Yoo-hoo, it's going to get cold."

From time to time you find yourself entertaining, around your table, other *Homo vedettus*, along with their little friends who like you, are fifteen years younger than their sweethearts. While the *Homo vedettus* merrily congratulate each other on their latest public appearances, and expatiate on the hopeless idiocy of journalists (nice for you, who are moving heaven and earth to become one!), the girlfriends exchange recipes and organize weekends in Las Vegas. When the members of his tribe have left your humble abode, the *Homo vedettus*, who to all appearances has enjoyed the evening, is seething with rage: this one has a swelled head, that one only talks about himself, a third can't admit that his last film was a flop. He is beside himself. He splutters. He gesticulates. He breaks out in a sweat. You offer him what is left of the pie or one last glass of port. That calms him down.

Note, however, that the right to criticize the members of his tribe is a privilege accorded only to the *Homo vedettus*. You are made aware of this one evening, when you dare to express some doubts concerning an actress's reputation.

"I'm not sure she's as deep as they say. I heard her this morning on the radio."

"How is the texture of your tartare, are you happy with it?"

"Yes, thank you."

"That girl is very nice. I know her."

"I'm sure she's *nice*. I didn't say she wasn't. But when she starts going on about how her trampoline course has changed her life, she comes across as a bit dim."

"And if you were the one who's dim?"

You exit the restaurant, leaving him with the bill. You should never feel guilty letting the *Homo vedettus* settle a bill. Not only does he earn the equivalent of your monthly salary in one morning of work, but above all, isn't it time you began saving your money for the therapy you'll need the day you're ready to get to the bottom of this whole affair?

He wears a cap and dark glasses, but when you find yourselves on streets he thinks are too busy, he seizes you by the arm and drags you into alleyways.

"Someone might recognize me. They might follow me home. They'd know where I live!"

You limp behind him in your high heels, cursing the puddles of water, the overflowing garbage cans, and the vagrants pissing against the wall. He accuses you of behaving like a princess. But try calling him paranoid and watch his reaction.

"I could cheat on you if I wanted to. I'm a public figure. Wherever I go, girls are always after me. I could have them by the shovelful. I already have. You should consider yourself lucky that I'm with you."

"So it's true what they said about you?"

"I'm a star. I score."

Everything is complex and confused. When things go wrong, a *Homo anonymus* goes for a walk and takes the air. At most, he goes to stay with friends for a few days. With the *Homo vedettus*, it's different. He buys a plane ticket to go and spend four days at a five-star Paris hotel. When he comes back, he announces that he's followed through on his threats with a woman he met in a Paris bar *who didn't even know who he was*. What are you supposed to think about that? That he has never before "made it" in the skin of a *Homo anonymus*? That doing so makes it more of a thrill?

You try not to make a big deal out of it, but you can't help seeing how far apart you are. And if the *Homo vedettus* is a creature who lives alone on a planet, certain that all the others are in orbit around his? Will there ever be room on that planet for another human being? You begin to doubt it.

So it is no accident that the *Homo vedettus* starts declaring more and more often that you don't understand him. And one day he throws you out. He helps carry your bags to the taxi. He kisses you. You are thirty years old.

"You're beautiful," he assures you. "But I've lost patience. I hope you won't lose too much weight because of your pain."

Try to see it as a liberation. *Homo vedettus* will no doubt return to the charge some months later in dramatic fashion, wanting your children. Try not to listen. And when you go shopping in your new neighbourhood where the lines at the grocery store are so long that you're again flipping through the magazines next to the cash, if by chance you happen on a photo of your *Homo vedettus*, stay calm. Gently stroke the glossy page, and tell yourself that that's it, his natural habitat — not the sheets of a conjugal bed.

Rebecca Leclerc was born in 1976. She lives in Montreal, where she works as a journalist. And you, are you married to a psychopath? To send us your texts, or to react to this column, visit www.pandoramag.ca

I shut the magazine and stared at an oval motif in the marble floor, but because it kept repeating itself like a stencilled pattern, the sight of it made me feel a little dizzy. My behind riveted to the squat armchair, I'd read the text twice, and still didn't know what to think; was I supposed to be amused by this account in the modern vein, whose writing had doubtless been therapeutic for my daughter, or should I rather deplore that such a large swath of her personal life was now in print in five, ten, fifteen thousand copies? Certainly, I'd never been much drawn to Simon, and the episode at the chalet didn't exactly endear him to me (by the way, I wondered, given that she was writing about all of Simon's failings, why did Rebecca say nothing about that day?), but I still questioned whether it was worth it for my daughter to dredge up a relationship that had been over for more than eighteen months. There was another matter, as well: why did she choose to call her friend rather than her mother when Simon let her down at the last minute? I felt a pang in my chest.

More and more guests were streaming out of the ballroom, passing along the corridor towards the lobby, and crowding into the revolving doors on their way to unknown destinations. I looked at my watch; the hands showed seven-fifteen. I went back into the ballroom. "Well," I tried to persuade myself, "if it did her some good to flush out the bad guy..." A group of girls was chattering away not far from the bar, all wearing the same dress with the neckline rimmed in green lace, like the hostess who was guarding the door when I arrived. There were not many people left, and it was easy for me to spot Rebecca; she was with a small group of people next to the windows with the heavy curtains. She was playing absent-mindedly with the tassel on one of the cords, and didn't seem to be following the conversation.

In the taxi making its way down Sherbrooke Street towards Park Avenue, Rebecca blew her nose, and pointed to the copy of *Pandora* sitting on my thighs.

"I wanted to surprise you!" she said. "That's why

I would have preferred us to be alone tonight. To celebrate the publication of my first piece that's more personal. More original."

The radio was tuned to the hockey game. I was thoughtful for a few seconds.

"But your novel about Mademoiselle Anne and her school in New France?" I ventured. "Have you abandoned it?"

Rebecca burst out laughing and the bulging eyes of the taxi driver met mine in the rear-view mirror.

"Mama, really!" sighed my daughter, finally.

"What?"

"I was twenty years old when I wanted to write that stupid book! I was brainwashed by *Les Filles de Caleb*!"

After giving me a sour look, Rebecca turned her head away and watched the street go by outside. I understood that we had stopped communicating. That often happens when I spend time with her. At first everything's fine; she's in a good mood. Then suddenly – most often when we're talking about something that concerns her, but sometimes for no obvious reason – she becomes detached, distant, foreign, and I have the impression that she's looking down on me, because everything I say is greeted only with cluckings of the tongue and sighs. "I don't understand why she shuts me out," I've often lamented to Pierre. "She's manipulating you," he answers, which I don't much appreciate, because what does he know? He was married twice before meeting me, but never had children. Still, when Rebecca becomes opaque like that, she leaves me with the unpleasant feeling that I've disappointed her, and it distresses me every time.

The neon signs along Sherbrooke Street shed a wan light onto the sidewalk. Just when, I wondered, did Rebecca change her mind about *Les Filles de Caleb*, that wonderful trilogy whose first two volumes I'd given her for Christmas so many years ago. Shut away in her bedroom, she'd devoured them in less than two weeks. For just an instant, I saw us again near the fireplace those winter nights, Valérie, Rebecca, and me, watching the television adaptation of the novels. Even Jean-Claude, when he wasn't held back at the office, joined us. As he'd grown up in the countryside, my husband appreciated the setting in which this drama played itself out: the thickness of the forests, the expanses of snow, the drowsy flatlands, the farm animals, the harvest in the fields, all that filled him with a feeling of nostalgia that I found hard to explain, given the haste with which he'd left his parents' land at the age of eighteen, never to return, except for his final repose.

The taxi braked suddenly. Rebecca and I had to grab at the seat so as not to be hurled forwards. The driver swore at the car that had just cut us off. I smoothed the sides of my dress, and Rebecca turned my way with an air of resignation that seemed to have hollowed out her cheeks.

"The thing is, Mama, that you can say it if you think my piece sucks. You don't have to like it."

"I found it very well written. It's full of, how do you say, crunch."

"Punch."

"There you are. But I still have the right to be afraid that you're doing the wrong thing by laying out your private affairs for all to see. Your personal life, especially when it's fragile, you have to protect it."

Rebecca shook her head, while undoing the scarf around her neck.

"I have a good insurance plan at the paper," she shot back. "I consulted a psychologist after my breakup with Simon. You know what he told me? That one of the reasons I let myself be treated like that was because you let yourself be dominated by Papa, and that's the only model I had."

I could hardly contain my indignation.

"Charlatan!"

"Okay, play the ostrich if you want!"

"And your sister Valérie, what about her? How do you explain that she has no problems with Marc? You both had the same model!"

"Hmmph."

"What?"

"Marc is a policeman! You don't think a cop is controlling, dominant?"

Was my daughter so unhappy that she wanted to pass on her delusions to all of us? I took a deep breath and tried to shift the conversation into a gentler mode.

"Did you never consider that you might just have had bad luck with Simon? It happens to everybody."

My daughter fixed me with a gaze that was both sad and sovereign, biting her bright red lips. "You're all I have," isn't that what she'd said on her thirtieth birthday? I felt like holding her to me.

"Think whatever you like," she murmured.

That was the last straw.

"Your father had his character and the problems we all know," I barked. "But under no circumstances, *none*, you hear me, would he have left me alone half-blind in the centre of the city. Never!"

I felt a sob rising up in my throat, but I quickly swallowed it down. The bulging eyes of the taxi driver were on me again, in the rear-view mirror. Glum, Rebecca just shook her head. "Wow!" she said, before turning her eyes towards the road once more. I assumed that the discussion was over. I didn't know what this "wow" meant, and I wondered if Rebecca believed a word of what she had said: that I was the source of her unhappiness in love, that I was the one who had predisposed her to it, precipitated it. That I had handed it down to her, like a hereditary defect.

"Oh, Murielle," I thought, while patting my hair above my neck, "you're lucky to have a boy."

Such a thing had never occurred to me before.

The dining room at Chez Gautier was full of life, with its clattering dishes, its conversations, its bursts of laughter, waiters shouting orders, and cell phones ringing. After having located my name in the reservations book, the maître d' took our coats and showed us the way to a table near the window. I sat down on the bench, and Rebecca headed for the bathroom. When she returned her hair was undone, and she seemed a little less sullen.

"I prefer the bench," she declared, sliding in beside me. "Raphaël will just have to sit in front of us!"

The moment I'd been waiting for for weeks was

about to arrive, to migrate from my fantasy world into reality. Suddenly, I was nervous. Fearful that silence would descend on us again, I told her how kind her neighbour had been to me earlier in the evening.

"Vincent gave you a lift to the Ritz!?" my daughter exclaimed.

The story seemed to amuse her, but its ending irritated her. Apparently Vincent was helpful by nature, and must have been very put off that I treated him like a common chauffeur in giving him twenty dollars.

So Rebecca called him immediately to make her excuses in my name, and while she left a message on his voicemail and I sipped my Chardonnay, I wondered if Vincent was not the mysterious Mister Condom. Why hadn't I thought of that earlier? What could prevent this man from climbing up to my daughter's whenever he felt like it? Even the nights he was looking after his children, once he had put them to bed, all he needed was one of those wireless surveillance monitors for him to mount with a clear conscience the few steps separating him from Rebecca, and to go back down to his daughters before they awoke, with no one the wiser.

Rebecca put her cell phone back on the table with a sigh.

"He seemed embarrassed, but not that much," I lied, remembering Vincent waving his arms in distress like a little bird. "And maybe he could buy you some flowers with the money, no?"

This was a not so subtle enticement to my daughter to come clean on the subject of her neighbour. Since she had told the story of her life in a magazine, why might she not confide in her mother?

"Come again?" she replied.

"You told me it had been ages since you'd received any."

My daughter smiled tightly.

"Okay, where's our friend?" she said, impatient. "We'll be drunk before he gets here if he takes much longer."

It was almost eight-fifteen and it's true that my head was beginning to spin from drinking like that on an empty stomach. We were just going to ask the waiter for a basket of bread when Raphaël finally appeared, and before the maître d' could even greet him, he spotted us and came over. He smiled shyly and played with the ring around his thumb.

"Sorry to be late," he said, once at our table, then he looked at me, adding, "Sharon, the girl at the gallery, you know? She called me in a panic an hour ago. She's been robbed and I went to her place to wait for the police."

"Oh, is she all right?"

"She's okay. They just turned everything upside down and took a whole bunch of stuff."

His head atilt, Raphaël finally took in Rebecca.

"Well, well..." he breathed, "how're you doing, you?"

"Good," she replied, chewing on the straw from her Bloody Caesar. "You?"

"I'm cool, yeah."

"Sit down," I said. "Take a seat!"

"We're getting pretty hungry!" said Rebecca.

Raphaël asked the waiter for a kir, and sat opposite Rebecca. While we were looking at our menus, I announced, over the top of mine, that dinner was on me. Raphaël had brought me the photo I'd asked him for, rolled in an elastic, and as Rebecca insisted on seeing it I opened it out on the table, and we were all able to admire the little monkey with his hand plunged into a bag of chips in the middle of the lush forest.

"I'm going to frame it and put it up in my new kitchen," I explained. Pierre had chosen white tiles, and I was afraid it would be too Swedish in style. This would add a bit of warmth.

"Why is he eating chips?" asked Rebecca. "Isn't there enough food in the forest?"

"The tourists have taken to feeding them," Raphaël replied, then he asked me, "Eighty dollars, is that okay?"

Rebecca kicked me under the table, but I ignored it; what else could I do? My daughter doubtless found Raphaël cheap for making me pay for the photograph when I had just said I was inviting them, and I must say I felt a bit that way myself, but how to know whether Raphaël might not have lost a certain amount of money with this business of the photo contest for a French magazine? Perhaps the costs of the inscription fee and the shipping were very onerous? It was certainly hard for him to live from his art, and eighty dollars, what would that change for me? The photos I saw exhibited the night before were going for more than a hundred dollars; of course, they were bigger and the price included the ebony-coloured frame, but why quibble? I thought of Murielle; Raphaël was her son, after all.

"Of course, my sweet, no problem."

Raphaël smiled with satisfaction.

"Great. Have you done something with your hair? It's not the same as yesterday."

I put the photograph down on the bench, next to my handbag. While Rebecca was deciding whether to take fries or a salad with her steak, Raphaël passed his eyes over her face, her hands, and her neckline. It occurred to me that it wasn't for nothing that Rebecca had taken her hair down a few minutes earlier; it was probably to please Raphaël. Were we already on the right track? I excused myself and went to the bathroom, where I wasn't able to do what I had intended because one of the toilets was blocked and the other out of service, which I did not think was worthy of this restaurant's reputation. It had been highly recommended to me by Brigitte Lemaître, the divorcée of easy virtue from my walking club, who claimed to have often encountered there well-known businessmen and politicians. I took my time all the same, adjusting my silver broach in front of the mirror, certain that being alone together would spark things happening between Rebecca and Raphaël.

When I got back, Raphaël was alone at the table. *Pandora* was open in front of him, covering the place settings, at a page I had no difficulty in recognizing. He was chewing on a piece of bread.

"She went to smoke a cigarette," he declared, interrupting his reading to fix me with a gaze that was rather stunned. "I wouldn't want to be in that guy's place!"

"That's our Rebecca," I said. "It's not without crunch."

"What?"

I dipped my lips into my glass.

The leek soup arrived just as Rebecca, still trailing fumes of nicotine, sat back down at the table. Until the main course was served, the conversation unfolded with various degrees of enthusiasm on subjects as diverse as the rarity of video clubs in the new neighbourhood to which Raphaël had moved, and the exorbitant rents where Rebecca was living. I put in my two cents' worth here and there with the occasional manifestation of surprise. It was only halfway through the meal that Rebecca, who seemed very relaxed by the wine, asked Raphaël what he thought of her text.

"You really want to know?" he asked, over his blood sausage.

"I'm interested. My mother's already told me she thought it sucks."

"I never said such a thing!"

Rebecca rolled her eyes and speared a few leaves of lettuce with her fork.

"First of all," Raphaël continued, in an irritable tone of voice, "it's nothing new. I know loads of women like you. How does it help you to be forever whining that we're all a bunch of egotists out to mistreat you?"

Rebecca didn't bat an eyelash. I trembled while peeling away a few threads of flesh from my lamb shank.

"It must help for something if they've published me!" replied my daughter.

At this point, there was a disturbance at the door to the dining room. A brawny young man and a girl, both dressed in red, white, and blue sweaters, were shouting, "Na-na-na-na-wey-hey-hey-good-bye!" A few customers applauded and raised their glasses in that direction. With the help of two waiters, the maître d' disposed of the intruders.

"In any case," Raphaël went on, once calm had been restored, "in India, women are much more modest than here."

"Really? In that case, why don't you marry one the next time you go down there?"

"Rebecca!" I interjected.

"What?"

Raphaël took a long drink of wine.

"If my ex were ever to pull a stunt like that, I'd have her in court before she knew what happened to her."

These weren't at all the sort of sparks I'd had in

mind. They were both tapping away at the keyboards on their cell phones, doubtless absorbed in sending those famous texts, when I proposed that we order chocolate profiteroles for dessert. It was suggested that I ask for the bill instead. That's what I did, and after I signed his cheque, Raphaël took his leave; he had to go back to Sharon, who was afraid of spending the night alone in an apartment that had been pillaged by thieves.

"Of course, I can't say no. We'll be in touch by e-mail, okay?"

As I watched him weave his way towards the exit between tables that were now mostly empty, I saw him again, a little boy on the beach, going beet red while protecting Rebecca and her sand castles from rambunctious toddlers. Wasn't he now doing the same thing, but for another?

"Do you think he's frustrated?" Rebecca asked.

"I don't know."

We'd finished our Grand Marnier.

"I think so, and it has nothing to do with tonight," my daughter said. "We ran into each other at a university party eight years ago, you understand?"

"Not really."

"We kissed."

"Oh."

"He left me a message two weeks later. *Two* weeks. I never replied. He wanted to go to the movies."

We stood up. My eyes clouded over while the maître d' was helping me on with my coat. "Oh Murielle," I thought, "that's where it leads when we let them cope all by themselves."

"Did you enjoy your evening?"

"Ah, your bathroom, Monsieur!" I protested, over my shoulder.

While Rebecca turned her back on me to find a taxi among the cars coming along Park Avenue in a symphony of honking horns, I felt my legs go weak and I had to grab onto a lamp post. How many reasons did I have to be dizzy? The failure of my plan, an enterprise, I realized, that had come much too late; the fact that Mademoiselle Anne no longer existed and that Rebecca was parading her personal life in public; the fact of not knowing who the man was who stuffed condoms in the garbage before leaving early in the morning; and finally the idea, however ludicrous, that I was perhaps the cause of all these misfortunes. But even more troubling was the urge I now felt to pull down the curtain on all of that, to stop worrying about it and to just go home. I would have liked to tell her, to shout it out, to stamp my foot on the pavement, both hands on my hips: "Rebecca, I want to go home! Let me leave!"

And yet, how to express this wish to my daughter without her feeling abandoned once and for all?

I went over to her.

"You just kissed?"

"Oh Mama," she implored.

"What?"

We climbed into a taxi and the car took off into the night.

Acknowledgments

Some of these stories have appeared in a somewhat different form in the literary reviews *L'Inconvénient*, *Zinc*, and *XYZ*, in the magazines *Madame* and *Urbania*, as well as the weekly *Ici*. I would like to thank the editors of those publications.

My thanks to the French Department of the University of Ottawa which, in the autumn of 2007, welcomed me as Writer in Residence.

For their wise judgment as first readers, a big thank you to Dominique Fortier, Yvon Rivard, India Desjardins, and Jean Bernier.

N.B.